Gichi Manidoo

Charles J. Musser

~

Every step we take on earth brings us to a new world.

–F. G. Lorca

DEDICATION

For E. The doors of the cage are open. Fly away to Capistrano, brave swallow, for all the mystery and splendor of the world await you.

Cover art and illustrations by Nancy Aphroditae

vii

CHAPTER ONE

Like a caballero's bag of gold

~Federico

When I first met Marie, I stood in the boiler room of an old house searching for documents to help my company sell the place.

Spanish waltzes drifted from the phone in my pocket. There was dust everywhere—in my eyes, up my nose, drying out my throat. I sneezed several times and wiped my nose on my sleeve. Out of the corner of my eye, I caught a shifting of shadows. Turning my head, I was surprised to find a woman standing there.

She was halfway down the stairs, and that would be how I always thought of Marie: halfway in this world and halfway out. I judged her to be in her early thirties. Thick, umber hair framed a face of dark complexion. A pair of Native American earrings dangled blue feathers that brushed her cheeks, and her eyes flashed.

It took a moment to find my voice. "Can I help you?"

She tilted her head. "Can *I* help *you*?"

"I'm sorry, miss, but you're trespassing."

"No, I'm not. I own this house."

I was at a loss. I distinctly remembered the man who'd instructed me in the sale of the house. He'd been barely courteous, as if being around other people was the last thing he wanted to do. His hands had been sweaty when he'd given me a curt handshake. With a pinched mouth, he'd said, "I don't much care for you, sir, so let's finish this, please." He'd looked past me, toward the road, as if he'd rather be anywhere else than standing next to me.

"I know Carl Mulligan owns this property," I said. "And you are his… daughter?" Her eyes narrowed and she frowned. "Sister?"

"I'm his wife, Marie."

"I'm sorry to hear that." I said it without thinking, and winced.

She flashed a slight smile and said quietly, "Thank you. And you are…?"

"Federico. Federico Garcia. I'm your realtor." As a large man, I know I can seem intimidating, so I tried my best to appear small and safe. I let my shoulders droop, tucked my goateed chin in a bit, and turned my body directly toward her.

She came the rest of the way down the stairs, stopping about six feet from me, and folded her arms. My phone played "*No Volveré.*" As it played, her body swayed to the slow, simple beat.

"You're a dancer?" I asked.

She stopped swaying and laughed. "I wish I was. I like to practice in the backyard. The music echoes off the old trees. It's much better than dancing in a stuffy studio." She looked through the grimy window high on the wall. I turned my gaze and saw a desiccated tree in the yard. "I used to dance with my brother. He and I would make them up and perform them for our parents, in front of the fire in winter and outside in the orchard in summer."

"I know how to waltz," I said, regretting my forwardness almost the moment the words passed my lips.

Our eyes locked and we stared at each other. "Someone taught me to waltz once, but it was a long time ago." Her face relaxed. It made me feel that she recognized me, that she remembered me from somewhere in her past. Yet that was impossible, for I was positive I had never seen her before. "Perhaps you can help me remember?" she asked.

To my surprise, I answered, "I'd love to." The song ended. "But unfortunately, we have no music." I could have simply replayed the song. I may have been a forty-year-old man, but I felt as shy and as awkward as a boy of fourteen.

She came closer and stood in front of me. Up close, her brown eyes had green flecks in them. They were beautiful. "Can't you hear the music around us?"

"I only hear the boiler," I said.

"Then you *can* hear it."

She reached out to take my hand. As we touched, the old boiler kicked in with a *bang*. I jerked, startling her.

"I'm sorry," I said. She nodded. The boiler crouched like a copper dinosaur between stacks of books and boxes. The flicker of a failing fluorescent light made it flash in and out of shadows.

So it was that I found myself with a married woman in my arms, dancing a waltz with the hushed percussion of steam.

"I'm not very good at dancing," I said. Nevertheless, I didn't have to think about the steps with Marie. It felt as if, although strangers, we had done this before. Nervous, I stepped on her toes. My expression must have given away my worry and embarrassment.

She brushed a stray strand of hair from my face. "It doesn't matter, Federico. It doesn't hurt."

One rainy day the following week, in a small café, we ate lunch and talked about her work as a nurse. She was in high spirits, radiant and playful. The smile on her face seemed to gather a cocoon of happiness around us that kept the rest of the gray world at bay. When I asked her about her husband, however, the smile faltered. It didn't disappear, it just became less real.

I pulled two theater tickets out of my pocket and set them next to her bowl of strawberry shortcake. She glanced at them.

"What's this?"

"A touring company production of a Broadway musical." I stirred a heaping teaspoon of honey in my tea and sipped. "*The Lion King.* Lots of talking and singing and dancing animals. You heard of it?"

"Of course I've heard of it." Ignoring her strawberries, she stared wide-eyed at the tickets. She picked one up and examined it. Setting the ticket down, she pushed them back toward my plate.

"They're gifts from a client," I explained. "I have a meeting that evening and can't attend. Take your husband. You give so much to your patients and to others, I wanted to give something to you." I folded a napkin into a bird's wing, laid it on top of the tickets and pushed them back toward her.

She looked away from the table, from the tickets, from me. "I can't. Besides, I'm really not interested in seeing a play."

I shrugged, scooped up the tickets and finished my tea-flavored honey.

She placed her hand on mine. "Carl doesn't like people. It's a phobia. And he's insecure, no matter how much he tries to portray himself as a tough-guy businessman. We love each other. It's just different than most other people, I think," she said.

"How is it different?"

"Others call him controlling and jealous. I know it for what it is. He's…protective."

I watched her face carefully. She wouldn't make eye-contact and her hands fidgeted with a fork. "How many friends do you have?" I asked.

"I have plenty of friends at work."

"How many friends can you go out shopping with? Have coffee with? See a movie with? Invite home for dinner or just plain hang out with? Tell me the truth—you'd love to see the play."

She stood to leave, the smile having vanished completely from her face. "I have to get back to work." I'd pushed too hard and regretted it. Hovering, she raised the fingers of her right hand to her lips.

"Yes?" I asked, standing up.

"If your meeting is canceled, and you go to the play, will you tell me about it?"

"Yes, of course I will. And if I see a decent dance step from a gazelle, I promise to show you."

She nodded. "Thank you. I'm not sure what animal I'd think of you as, but a gazelle is not among the choices, Fede."

"No?" I raised an eyebrow, put my hand over my head like a flamenco dancer, and spun around in a tight circle on the ball of my foot next to our table, knocking over a glass of water. I watched the water drip from the edges of the tablecloth as scattered applause came from the café's patrons.

I bowed to Marie. She smiled again.

"I'll see you tomorrow," she said with a nod.

The next morning, a Saturday with her husband away on a business trip, we went on a jaunt to a mountain about 20 minutes from the city. It was a stunning autumn day, the air crisp and pure. Dressed in jeans and a yellow sweater, her hair up, she followed me along a winding path that led to the top.

We crested the peak, a small plateau wrapped in a cloudless sky. Conifers grew around us, and one lone oak tree stood near the ledge overlooking a crimson-painted forest and farmland below.

Marie walked near to the edge, her back to me. Her proximity to the precipice before us was unnerving. I stepped close behind her, placed my hands on her shoulders, and gazed over the steep cliff.

She leaned back into my arms, then drew them tightly around her. "What if we stepped off the edge? Would we fall, or fly away?"

"My money would be on falling, but my heart would be on flying. I grew up in the mountains, you know. I've always felt connected to them."

"Oh? Where?"

"New Mexico. The Sangre de Cristo range near Santa Fe."

"I see. How were you connected? What did they mean to

you?"

I had to think about that. "I was raised an orphan. My father was killed by the cartel in Guadalajara, Mexico, and my mother immigrated here and had me."

"That's terrible."

I shrugged. "I never knew him. Then she died when I was eight, and I ended up in the foster care system. Anyway, the mountains were silent. They were powerful and magical. They didn't need to be loud and aggressive to be strong. Unlike the men that hung around *mi madre*."

"What was her name?"

"Marianela." I rested my chin on the top of her head.

"Such a beautiful name."

"It is." After a few minutes, I pulled her away from the edge and released her. She ran to the oak tree and scrambled up to a heavy, low-hanging branch. I paused at the base, my arms folded.

"I'm not a monkey, I'm afraid."

She laughed. "You've never climbed a tree? If you start to fall, I'll catch you."

"Uh huh. Fine. If the branch breaks off, I'll visit you in the hospital." I climbed and pulled myself to a precarious position, straddling the thick branch. I shuffled up close behind her once again. Like dampened ferns in the rain, she settled once again into my arms, her back to me and her sweater bunched at my mouth. I pushed it down and kissed the nape of her neck. She shivered.

I couldn't get my bearings or think straight. I knew she was another man's wife, that this was wrong, but I also knew this intimacy was the mountain, the air, the living magic of the world itself that kept me there and holding her.

She ran her fingers over my bicep and then inner forearm, tracing a green-and-ruby colored tattoo. "A rose—how lovely." She counted the petals with her fingernail. "Twelve."

I rolled my arm back over. She turned to look at me, a soft smile on her lips. "A lover?"

I shook my head.

"Lovers?" she asked and winked.

"It has nothing to do with love."

She frowned, then turned the back of her head to me once again and whispered, "Will you recite your poem? The one you've been working on?"

"I told you, it's no good. You'll hate it."

"The truth is what I say it is," she replied, imitating my annoyed tone.

I took a deep breath and grimaced. I hated the sound of my voice.

> The sky is filled with a weep
> of anthers. The poplar's branch
> hangs my straw hat, the river-fog unfurls

like a quilt's promise of dreams

and over the bristle-grass the moon,
a bell in black-bled stillness, rings
ripe with crazy promise
like a caballero's bag of gold.

We lie in the earth's first morning,
ruffed like arrow-feathers,
your dark hair turned to me,
and become Hyacinth blossoms.

Beyond us, the fox flames.
The owl on its wing
hunts the meadow vole,
the thickets fade as rain,

and a stallion, all hoof
and rib, stands like iron
in the young sun,
pinned by your eyes.

After a few moments of silence, she said, "Yes, it sucks
horribly, Fede."

I chuckled.

A gunshot exploded from a nearby stand of trees. I almost
fell from the branch, but she turned and grabbed my shoulders
with both hands and pulled me back to a shaky balance. We
clung to each other as the blast echoed. I squeezed my eyes
shut, fighting the cellular-level memory of buried IEDs,
incoming mortar fire…

My tour in Afghanistan rushed back, and a darkness bubbled to the surface once again. I pushed it down as best I could.

A gut-shot buck bolted from the pine trees at a full run toward our perch, like an arrow from the mountain's shadow. It halted directly below us. Its snout and rack scattered dirt up to the sky, and then it collapsed.

We climbed down. The hunter was nowhere in sight. I held my arm around Marie's waist and she clung to my shirt as we watched the animal take its last, labored breath.

She lifted her face to me. "I think we should leave," she said. I held her hand and led her toward the winding path.

A man walked out from the dense brush, a rifle propped over the back of his neck, both arms braced over barrel and stock, and a smirk on his face. He was in his early twenties with long hair and full beard, a red baseball cap on his head. He stopped in front of the buck, hacked, and then spat on the ground. We stared at him.

"What the hell are you looking at?" he asked.

Something inside me clicked. I'd met this attitude and this man in many guises before. Marie put her hand on my arm as I stepped forward.

"Let's go, Fede," she whispered. "Please."

I smiled at Marie. "Everything's fine," I said to her, then walked casually up to the man. I stopped about six feet in front of him. He took one step back and jutted his chin.

"Hunting season isn't for another month," I said, holding his gaze. I gestured at the rifle. He flinched. "Carrying a weapon like that is dangerous to others." He slowly swung the rifle out and down to his side, barrel pointed to the ground.

"What business is it of yours? Take your lady and get out of here." As he spoke, he raised the barrel just a little, so it pointed toward my left foot. He grinned at me.

I took another step forward, holding his eyes with mine. There was now no more than three feet separating us. The rifle rose another foot, pointing at my mid-section.

"Fede," Marie called loudly. I ignored her. I felt the strangeness rise in me, the warrior, the wolf and wolverine, the long teeth, the razor claws. As I stared in his eyes, I sensed a tremble run along his arm to his fingers on the rifle. It was fear, and I knew it well—an old friend.

I couldn't stop what happened next. I tried, I fought against it, but it happened so quickly that I felt at home once again—I knew who I was for a few brief seconds.

Making sure his finger wasn't on the trigger, I grabbed the barrel, stepped to the side, twisted, placed my other hand on the stock between his hands and forced the barrel down then up in one lightning circle. The motion broke his grip, and the barrel smashed up into his groin with a thud. He stumbled back, coughing, and holding his crotch.

I carefully examined the rifle, popped the magazine, and ejected the round. He ran back into the bushes from where he came. I strolled until I was next to the buck, tossed the magazine into the bushes, and then jammed the rifle deep into the ground, barrel first, above the deer's proud rack. It all happened in the space of about ten seconds, although at the end I felt as weary as if it had taken a lifetime.

I took a deep breath and relaxed my shoulders. Marie stared at me as I walked up to her.

We stood in silence.

"You reminded me of *him*, for just a second," she said quietly.

"I'm sorry. I should have let it go." I looked down at my feet as I stood in front of her. She took my hand and held it.

"It's okay. We all make mistakes."

We turned together and went down the mountain. Despite my best efforts, she'd caught a glimpse of the stranger inside me.

Near the bottom, she stopped and turned to me, gazing into my eyes as if searching for something. "I can't leave him, you know. He wouldn't survive it. He loves me in his own way, and I love him in mine."

I frowned and opened my mouth to reply, but she shook her head. I wanted to tell her, *leave him before…* I opened my mouth to speak.

"Don't. Please." She stepped forward and kissed my cheek. We hugged. "Don't say anything," she whispered. She hurried off to her car. I watched until all I saw were her taillights as she sped away.

We had begun a regular morning ritual. We would meet before work at a small wooden park bench amid towering pine trees. The bench sat at the end of a dirt path overlooking a small lake. I always brought two coffees, one for her with double soy milk and no sugar, and one for me, black with three packets of honey. We would sit watching the sun rise above the trees on the other side of the lake.

The maple trees had begun their annual turn to russet and orange in Michigan. The sunlight flickered and dappled across her face. I reached in my pocket for my phone and asked if I could take a picture of her.

"Please don't." Since our time on the mountain a few days earlier, she had grown distant and distracted.

"But it would make such a beautiful picture," I said. "I could send it to you."

"I don't bring my phone here. Carl uses an app to keep tabs on me. He wouldn't approve of my being here with you." She averted her eyes, drank her coffee, and set the empty cup on the ground beside her.

I raised an eyebrow. "He keeps tabs on you?"

"He worries about me," she replied, her fingers fidgeting in her lap. "He wants me to be safe."

"Then perhaps we shouldn't be…"

She turned quickly and gave me a brilliant smile. "No. I enjoy our talks, Federico. And our dances. You tell such lovely stories. It's obvious you're a writer at heart." Blushing softly, she stared down at her hands. "It's just that… it's true that he doesn't allow me to have any friends, but it's because he's so protective. He wants me to be safe."

"Yes, safe." I stared at my coffee and ran my finger around the edge of the paper cup.

This vibrant woman sitting next to me is living in a cage, I realized. I wondered if she understood how twisted that made Carl's love. *The lies we tell ourselves are the worst kind.*

She put her hand on my arm, and I turned to smile at her. *Don't go home tonight,* I wanted to say.

"Will I see you tomorrow?" I asked, instead.

"Of course!" She reached into my shirt pocket, snatched my phone, and played "*No Volveré.*" Since that day in the boiler room, it had become our song. She placed it back into my pocket and stood. I rose with her and we waltzed in the brisk autumn air.

When the song finished, she pulled back and looked in my eyes. "Don't worry about me. I'm an adult and can take care of myself."

She turned, hesitated, and then gave me a quick kiss on the cheek. Before I could say anything, she called over her shoulder, "*Adios*, Fede," and disappeared around a bend in the path.

CHAPTER TWO

Déjà ressenti

~Federico

I arrived the next morning with coffees in hand as usual. The sky had turned gray and weighed heavily on the lake. I waited for about 30 minutes, and checked my phone for the third time, but there were no messages. Marie never came. I considered texting her. She was busy, I assumed, so I left for work.

I returned the next day. She didn't show up again. I began to worry. I stared at my phone, nearly ready to call her.

"She can't answer," said a soft female voice. I looked up from my seat on the bench, startled. The voice came from a teenage girl dressed in a red t-shirt and faded blue jeans, her hands jammed in her jean pockets. Her black hair was cut short and she stood in the shade of a tall tree. Around her neck hung a dreamcatcher made of beads and feathers.

"Are you talking to me?" I asked.

She walked closer and sat down beside me on the other end of the bench.

A flock of geese flew in over the treetops and skimmed the

lake's surface settling near the shore.

We sat in silence as I stared at her.

"I'm Elizabeth."

Her right hand was balled in a fist. She tapped it against her thigh gently.

"Marie is dying," she said matter-of-factly.

"What?" My fingers loosened and the coffee in my cup sloshed on my leg.

"But you can help her, Federico." She put her hands together and pressed her fingertips to her lips.

"Where is she? Is she in the hospital?"

Elizabeth nodded. She fingered a long feather that hung from the dreamcatcher. On the lake, one of the geese beat the water into a froth with its wings. "But that doesn't matter."

"What do you mean, it doesn't matter? What happened to her? And how do you know my name?" I stood, began to pace, and ran my fingers through my hair.

"She wants me to tell you what happened to me. And for you to believe it."

I stopped pacing. "She wants me to listen to a story from you? Told to me by a strange girl I've never met before?"

"Yes. She wants you to listen and believe."

I stared into her eyes. I could have sworn I knew her, but I'd never seen her before. Something about her eyes—it's always the eyes that bring us in or keep us out.

I shook my head. "Who are you, and how do you know Marie?" I gripped the bench with both hands, trapping her between my arms. "Are you her daughter? Her sister?"

"She doesn't have a daughter. And no, I'm not her sister." She turned her gaze to the geese, and I stepped back. A cloud of orange and crimson leaves fell around her, like dying butterflies.

I turned and headed down the path. I needed to end this now before I fell any further down a rabbit hole and couldn't climb out. Was she lying? How did she know me? Did Carl find out I'd been meeting with Marie and hurt her?

From behind me, a familiar melody began to play. I spun around. Elizabeth was holding up a cellphone, *"No Volveré"* playing loudly from its speaker.

I returned to the bench and sat down next to her.

"It's such a pretty melody," she said and pointed to the flock of geese.

The geese circled each other, stopping every few beats to spin in a circle all their own in unison. I sat there, mesmerized.

To my astonishment, I realized they were no longer geese at all, but swans. I blinked twice, yet still they held to their new, dignified forms. When I looked back at her, one of the feathers on the dreamcatcher glowed. I stared from it, to her face, to the swans. For just a moment, this all seemed familiar. It wasn't déjà vu, but *déjà ressenti*. Already felt.

"If I listen to your story, and believe it, you say it will help her?"

She nodded. "And you have to tell the story, too. You've got to tell—"

"And who am I supposed to tell the story to?"

"You're a poet, a writer."

"How do you know I'm a writer? And how will it help her? At least tell me that."

"You're not supposed to be so annoying." Her eyes flashed at me. "This is *not* the way I want things to go."

She stood and strode toward the lake. With her arms wrapped around her, her silhouette against the sunlight looked so lonely, as if a fawn had wandered off and lost its mother. I went to stand next to her, arms folded.

"Tell me how listening to your story can help Marie. Then maybe I'll do as you ask."

She tilted her head as if looking for the right words.

"You won't understand this now," she began. "When I'm done, you will. But if you believe me, Marie will have a new life. She'll be free again."

I closed my eyes and took a deep breath. I considered walking away but according to this strange girl, Marie's well-being hung in the balance.

"When do we start?" I asked.

"I can't stay longer today, but I'll be here tomorrow.

Someone needs me now. Don't forget."

"I have a great memory."

"I don't." She turned, walked up the path, and disappeared into the shadows.

Once home, I searched the local news online and found what I was looking for. Normally, a story like this didn't warrant a news brief, but Marie's husband was wealthy and powerful. The report said that a Marie Mulligan had fallen down a flight of stairs into a boiler room and suffered a severe head injury. Now comatose and in critical condition, she was in the ICU of Mt. Pleasant Hospital. When police questioned her husband, he told them she had tripped and fallen.

I slept very little that night, thoughts of Marie lying in a hospital bed running through my mind. Rising before the sun, I grabbed my notebook, stopped to purchase a coffee and an orange juice, and then headed to the park. I arrived just as the sun slipped above the horizon, and Elizabeth was there as promised. Her clothes were the same. Jean cuffs rolled up, she waded in the shallows of the lake among the swans, a pair of sneakers dangling from her fingers. I was surprised the swans tolerated her presence. She noticed me approaching, waved, and climbed up the bank toward me.

She set her worn sneakers on the bench beside her and pulled the heels of her muddy feet up to its edge, wrapping her arms around her knees.

"Good morning, Elizabeth," I said as I sat beside her. I handed her the orange juice.

"Oh, no thank you. I like coffee."

I offered her mine, but she shook her head. I shrugged and took a quick sip of coffee.

"Ready?" she asked.

"*Si, Señorita. Vamos.*" I took out my notebook.

"Vamos?"

"Let's go."

She cleared her throat and once again fiddled with one of the long feathers from the dreamcatcher hanging around her neck. I was startled to see a silver meerkat push its way through heavy grasses not far behind her. It jumped up on the bench beside her, watching me carefully. I smiled warily, resigned to another manifestation of the strange world I was falling into, and nodded. Satisfied, the animal looked away and groomed itself as Elizabeth spoke.

"It all started when I woke up and couldn't remember who I was or where I came from," she began.

CHAPTER THREE

I was hoping I could free her

~*Elizabeth*

Elizabeth walked out of the darkness beside a stream. She didn't know where she was or how she got there. The stream flowed across a path carved in the woods. Although all was quiet and peaceful, something was wrong.

My name is… She couldn't remember. Her name started with an 'E,' she somehow knew, but knowing one letter was hardly reassuring. Her breath caught in her throat as she skirted the razor edge of panic.

She stared at the sky. It was the deepest shade of sapphire. So absorbed in the color, she stepped in a hole and went sprawling. She caught herself with both palms on the ground, the shock running through her arms to her shoulders. Small mounds of fresh dirt like a burrowing animal might leave lay around the edges of the hole. Taking a deep breath, she climbed out and rolled her eyes. Her chest tightened. Crawling to the stream, she washed the dirt from her hands.

White-knuckled, she curled her fist around a maple sapling and gazed into the stream. A school of minnows swam in an eddy. They were silver and flashed sparks of bright orange. The sparks shot back and forth, like thousands of flickering stars. *They're talking to each other*, Elizabeth thought. She cocked her head to listen. She could make out a soft whisper. Her breathing slowed, and her shoulders relaxed.

She stared at her image on the water's surface, distorted by ripples, curious about what she looked like. Curly, charcoal hair framed a face of dark complexion, mahogany eyes, and accented with a small nose. Her lips, while pursed and tightened now, relaxed into an impish half-smile. She twitched her nose, not recognizing it. It was hers, all right. She bobbed her head up and down—the curls of her hair bounced like unwound springs. She stuck her tongue out, tried to lick the end of her nose, but couldn't quite reach…

"I guess that really is me, then," she said quietly, turning away, only to startle at the sight of a long, slender animal sitting in the grass. The creature was handsome, about the size of a house cat with shining black eyes that stood out from dark rings in its elongated face. More dark markings ran crosswise down the length of its back, a sharp contrast against the rest of its short silvery coat, before coming to an end at the tip of its long tail.

The creature folded stubby front legs across a puffed chest in an effort to appear bigger. Elizabeth matched its pose, and the pair regarded one another. It reminded her of a mongoose or perhaps a mink.

"Well?" she said.

"I see you," said the animal. Its nose twitched.

She gave a start. A talking animal meant she *had* to be dreaming. "I should think you can. I'm standing right here, after all."

"And why are you here, human girl?"

She tried to reach back in the darkened corridors of her memory, looking for something, some scrap from before the time she walked out of the darkness. There was only a locked door.

"You're not supposed to be able to talk, you know. And I don't know why I'm here. I think I might be lost. I can't remember where home is or how to get there," she said, tapping her fist against her thigh to help her wake up.

Nothing seemed magical or dreamlike in her surroundings. Except for the talking animal, of course. "And whispering fish," she said out loud.

The animal sat back on its haunches and, using its tail for balance, stood almost straight. It wiggled its little nose. "Of course fish can whisper. And how can you be lost? You're right here."

"But I don't know where here is."

The animal scratched at its whiskers. "*Here* is where here is. You are where you are. And if you are where you are, you'll never be lost."

"I suppose," she agreed reluctantly. She could see the logic behind his words, but still she'd have felt better if she'd known where she was and how she'd come to be here. She met its gaze. "Do you have a name, Mr. Mongoose?"

The animal pulled itself straighter still. "I most definitely am *not* a mongoose. I am a meerkat. And my name is Zaagitoon. But you may call me Zaagi. I am very rare."

"That I can agree with. I don't think I've ever met a talking meerkat, or a meerkat of any kind."

"Then you are lucky you've met me, human girl."

"So it appears. I'm pleased to meet you, Zaagi."

"I should think so," said Zaagi. He came closer, pressing through the tall grass, sniffing. "What's your name?"

"Elizabeth," she said without thinking, then frowned at how easily it had come to her. She hoped everything she wanted to know would turn up in her head in the same manner. "At least I think that's my name." She shrugged. "I may as well keep it for now."

"And what does that face mean?" Zaagi asked.

"What face?"

Zaagi wrinkled his nose, narrowed his eyes, and flattened his ears. "The one like this."

"Oh, you mean when I frown," said Elizabeth, repeating the expression. "When I do that, it means I don't know what to say."

"Why not just say that?"

She placed her hands on her hips and glared at Zaagi. "Fine. How about I say this, then. I can't remember anything, I'm scared, and I don't have time for talking animals. I'm dreaming, obviously, and it's about time I woke up."

Zaagi bobbed his head. "That's better, for I can see you mean it. If you are dreaming and want to wake up, start meaning things you say. Frowning is for dreamers, I think. Where is your mob?"

"My mob?"

"Yes. Your clan, your family. Your mob."

"I don't know. And I don't know where my home is."

He moved closer and sniffed at her, his little black nose twitching. "You look and smell ancient. How many summers have you seen?"

"I'm not sure." She looked at her body, not at all surprised that she couldn't remember how old she was. "Maybe fourteen?" The knowledge didn't arrive in her head the same way her name had, but there was something that just seemed right about that number.

Zaagi wrinkled his nose. "That's old. I've seen three summers, and I'm fully grown-up." He paced back and forth and cocked his head, as if pondering what she had said. "Are you going to die soon?" He took a step back, as though he expected her to keel over at any moment.

"I'm still young." She grimaced and plopped down in the grass.

Zaagi shuffled beside her and plopped down as well. "Humans live too long."

"Too long for what?"

"Too long to care about their hearts." Zaagi pointed. "Look at the stream. Where does it end?"

"I don't know."

"Exactly. You are too sure it won't stop tomorrow to care about it. Dying makes us rare. If we were here forever, and knew it, we wouldn't take notice of important things, which are always the things of the heart." Zaagi flicked his whiskers. "You're frowning again."

Elizabeth made the most severe frown she could, squinting, pursing her lips, and furrowing her brow.

"Like *that*," Zaagi said, pointing. "That's a good one."

Elizabeth relaxed her face and rolled her eyes.

Zaagi rose and jumped back and forth, muttering, "What to do with her. Leave her? Take her? Take her, then leave her?" He spun in a circle and stopped. "I know someone who might be able to give you some answers. Would you like me to bring you to him?"

Elizabeth closed her eyes, struggling to remember, to grasp even a grain of an image from a former life. But nothing rose in her mind's eye except emptiness.

Upper lip quivering, she turned away from Zaagi, fighting the urge to cry. Something had been there once, where the emptiness now resided. Like love.

There had to be people who missed her. There had to be *someone.*

With the type of assurance only an aching heart could give, Elizabeth made a decision. She would chase this dream, or whatever it was, wherever it led. She *would* find a way home.

She faced Zaagi again, determination steeling her spine. "I would love your help, my friend."

"Then follow me." Zaagi hopped once and looked over his shoulder. "Come on."

"Why do I have to follow you?" she said playfully. "Can't we go side by side?"

Zaagi nodded. "Just so! We will push the Luck-Boulder up the hill together, as they say around here. But if we're not careful, the boulder will roll back down and squash us into human-meerkat puddles."

Elizabeth laughed. "I don't know who I am, but I know I'm not likely to be squashed by *anything* without a fight, that's for sure." She ran her fingers through her hair and shook her head.

"The Unsquashable Elizabeth." Zaagi smoothed back both ears with his paws and shook his head too. It seemed to Elizabeth that he tried to raise an eyebrow as well but when that failed he gave up and bowed.

Elizabeth nodded, and the two walked along the stream until they came across a pathway with a rickety wooden bridge that crossed it. They joined the path then passed over the bridge and walked up a hill that turned from forest to meadow. She trailed her hand along the tops of yellow, purple, and red daisies. The petals were soft against her fingertips.

Above a cluster of yellow blooms she felt movement,

yanked her hand back and stopped. She put both palms out a few inches above the blossoms and waved them in a slow circle. The flowers followed her hands, reaching for them.

"Zaagi! Look!"

"They're only flowers," Zaagi muttered. "No need to get so excited about them." Despite his grouchiness, he stopped and sniffed a small, pale blue flower hanging face-down from its stem, looking like the bottom half of a floor-sweeping skirt.

"That's a beautiful one," she said softly. "What's it called?"

"A bellflower," Zaagi said reverently. With the tip of his paw, he nudged the blossom until it swung like a little chime in the wind. "I had a friend called Bellflower."

Elizabeth saw how his little head sagged. "You *had* a friend?" she asked gently.

Zaagi's head sunk all the way to his furry chest. "She'll never return to me."

"I'm so sorry." She knelt and stroked his back. His fur was the finest silk beneath her palm.

"She's locked in a cage. I was hoping I could free her."

"Is that why you were by the stream?"

He shook his head, and his old irritable tones returned. "No, I was waiting to meet someone who could help me. But then you came along and scared him away."

"I did? Maybe if we go back?"

"No. He won't be back. But don't worry, he's never far

away."

"If I scared your friend away, then I'll help you instead until he comes along. It seems only fair."

"I didn't say he was my friend. He's no one's friend." Elizabeth could see a shiver under Zaagi's fur as he said the words.

"But he was going to help you free Bellflower."

"I didn't say that either. I said he was going to help me."

"Well, I'll help you free Bellflower. I was locked in a cage once, and I'll never go back." Elizabeth stopped and arched her brow. "What a strange thing to say. Have I been in a cage?"

Zaagi shook himself like he was casting water from his fur. He glared at her. "If you insist on doing out-loud thinking, take it behind a bush, or in your case a tree. That's where we do our private things, thank you very much." He loped off, calling over his shoulder, "If you want to meet someone who can help you, you'll have to hurry."

Zaagi kept moving forward, not looking back. Elizabeth scrambled to her feet and hurried after him.

When she caught up, Zaagi sniffed in a distasteful manner. "You run wrong."

"You jog wrong." She grinned and the meerkat frowned. She looked behind her at the stream. Her heart thrummed in her chest and worry twisted her guts. She'd come in that way—

what if it was the way out too? What if she was going in the wrong direction? Her step faltered.

Ahead of her, Zaagi called out, "Keep up, little human."

With a deep breath, Elizabeth rolled her eyes, turned her back on the stream, and followed her new companion into an unknown world.

CHAPTER FOUR

Turn for turn and twist for twist -Kipling

~Elizabeth

At the end of the meadow of flowers, Elizabeth and Zaagi came upon a field of wild strawberries. She knelt to pick some berries, cupping them in one hand. She ate them and when she had finished, she wiped the juice on her pant legs. "Would you like one?"

"Hardly. Only starving meerkats would eat a strawberry."

"Well, what do you like to eat?"

Zaagi pawed the dirt wistfully. "Scorpions. But I haven't found any in this place."

"*Scorpions?* Oh my."

"I know, they're lovely, yes? But there are none to be found. I manage with beetles and centipedes and snakes."

Elizabeth made a gagging face but hid it from Zaagi by turning her head away. "How much farther?"

"It is far." He squinted at the sky. "We should resume our journey if we're going to make it there before nightfall."

Elizabeth stared at the cloudless blue sky. The hot sun warmed her face. She yawned and said, "I'm tired." Her eyelids were heavy.

"I would like to return to our journey," Zaagi said.

"And I'd like to nap," Elizabeth replied, mimicking Zaagi's annoyed tone. "Please?" She lay down among the strawberries.

Zaagi sat beside her and wiggled his nose in triumph. "Aha! How can you be sleepy if you're dreaming, hmmm?" He folded his arms across his chest, waiting.

Elizabeth narrowed her eyes. "Maybe... there are dreams inside other dreams?"

At this, Zaagi sighed and rolled on his back, feet twitching in the air. "Still, you persist. Oh, very well. If we must nap, though it's an idle thing to do, may I at least sleep on your stomach? It looks soft."

As they settled in the warm sun, a thick and heavy stench washed over them, smelling like raw sewage. Elizabeth gagged and covered her mouth. Zaagi rolled over, stuck his nose into the dirt and rubbed it back and forth.

Three giant vultures, wings flapping, settled to the ground, surrounding them. Viscera and blood covered their scarlet heads and hooked beaks. Elizabeth got to her knees and grabbed Zaagi, pulling him into a tight, protective hug.

Zaagi pulled away from her hug and stood on his hind legs, looking at each bird in turn. He made loud, chattering noises through exposed sharp teeth. "Come closer and die," he said. The birds scratched at the ground with their talons, but kept their distance after Zaagi's warning.

"What should we do?" asked Elizabeth.

"No holes nearby, so we stand and we fight," hissed Zaagi from the side of his mouth.

One of the vultures lifted its wings like a skirt, hopped forward on its clawed legs then settled again. The other two followed suit, closing in on Zaagi and Elizabeth. Each was at least a foot taller than she was.

Elizabeth held her stomach and dry-heaved from the stink. She steadied herself. "Should we run?"

"Run away? Who are you?"

"Who am I?" Elizabeth's eyes flashed at Zaagi as she repeated his question.

"What happened to Unsquashable Elizabeth?"

Elizabeth shook her head hard. The stench made thinking difficult.

The nearest vulture lunged and snatched Zaagi in its wings. It tossed him six feet into the air. Zaagi tumbled end over end and landed with a soft plop in the grass at Elizabeth's feet.

"Ow!" yelled Zaagi.

Zaagi righted himself and shot forward. His needle teeth sunk into a tuft of feathers and he yanked them out of the vulture's leg. The vulture squawked and hopped back a few feet. Zaagi spat the bloody feathers to the ground.

"Did you see that? I thought he would bounce more," said

the Front Vulture to the others. Zaagi seemed dazed, but okay.

"Stop that right now!" Elizabeth yelled. "Leave us alone and go away, or—"

The Behind Vulture cackled, "You're just a confused bag of blood. Shut your beak."

The Side Vulture croaked, "We have big plans for both of you."

"Pipe down, idiot," said the Behind Vulture to the Side Vulture. "You're going to give away our plan to eat them."

Elizabeth jammed her fists into her hips. "You certainly *aren't* going to eat us. What do you want?"

"We demand, we demand… Oh, I can't remember," said the Front Vulture. "Let's just eat them."

"Maybe we should eat *you*," said the Side Vulture to the forgetful Front Vulture, hopping up and down and pointing his wing at him. "That's a tasty plan." As he spoke, the Front vulture cowered.

"No, no, that's a stupid plan," said the Behind Vulture to the Side Vulture. "He won't taste good—he's stringy-old, and fatless." He looked at Elizabeth and Zaagi. "Those are the tasty-good and plump dinners. Time to slice and rip." The Behind Vulture lifted his head to the sky and let out a piercing scream, and the other two joined him.

"Why don't you go away, all three of you?" Elizabeth said. "I thought you only eat dead things, anyway."

The Behind Vulture screeched, "She knows our plan! She knows our beautiful idea to eat undead blood bags!"

Elizabeth lowered her head, narrowed her yes, and glared at the vultures. She clenched her fists and raised an arm. "If you don't beat it, I'll knock you all on your feathered butts."

Zaagi glanced at Elizabeth then looked back at the vultures. His eyes widened and his jaw hardened. "Yes. She has smacking hands. They'll sting you worse than the Diamond

Snake or fire's dancing ruby feathers."

Glaring at Zaagi and Elizabeth, their beaks snapping, the vultures closed in. The Side Vulture lunged at Elizabeth and tore at her forearm. She screamed and swung her fist at its head. There was a loud thump as it fell on its side, wings splayed. Blood dripped from Elizabeth's lower arm. It burned like a flaming match held against her skin. The vulture flapped his wings hard and pulled himself up as Elizabeth wiped the blood on her jeans. When she looked up again, all three vultures descended on them, wings spread, forming a barrier between their bodies and escape.

"I have a plan," said Zaagi. "But first…" There was a warm whoosh against Elizabeth's leg as Zaagi flashed forward at a vulture. It raised its talons. Elizabeth froze. Zaagi was headed into its sharp grasp. She saw a silver blur, the vulture shrieked, and Zaagi was at her side again. He'd bitten off more of the vulture's bloody feathers.

"You're *fast.*" Elizabeth raised her eyebrow. "What plan?" She picked up a handful of dirt, tossed it in the eyes of a nearby bird that had tried to sneak up behind her, and kicked at it. Her foot landed solidly on the side of its head, sending blood spatters flying. The vulture crumpled to the ground, its wings jerking spasmodically.

"You fight like a meerkat, human girl. I'd be honored to be in your mob. Now distract them." Zaagi put his face into the dirt and began to dig. Clumps of earth and small rocks flew out between his legs.

"Distract them? *How?*" whispered Elizabeth. Zaagi ignored her. A shadow shot toward her as a vulture swooped in low to the ground with his claws raised. She pivoted and kicked at its face. The loose mound of dirt shifted. She stumbled back, tripped over a clump of strawberry plants, and fell onto her behind. The vulture missed and veered sideways. She looked up as it crashed into the ground.

More dirt flew as Zaagi nearly disappeared into the hole, only the tip of his bobbing tail visible. All three birds closed in, the stench as thick as rotting gruel. Elizabeth stood and looked around frantically. The vultures surrounded them again, blotting out the sunlight. There was no way Zaagi could dig fast enough for a human being to dive into a hole. Elizabeth glanced around, desperate to find an opening to run.

"Oh. Oh. Look over there." Elizabeth pointed toward a stand of birch trees. "The meerkat's escaping to the other end of his hole. You should all go over there." All three birds whipped their heads around. "Quick, quick, he's getting away!" she yelled. All three vultures squawked and launched themselves into the air, feather-down floating in their wake, toward the trees to which Elizabeth pointed.

She looked down. Zaagi was gone. Just a hole remained, barely wider than her waist, she estimated. "Zaagi?" she yelled into the hole. Silence. She dropped to her knees and peered into the darkness. Although the dirt was soft, she was amazed that Zaagi could dig such a large hole so quickly. Her heart thumped faster. She took a deep breath to yell for him again as Zaagi's head popped up. She looked up. The birds, about fifty yards distant, had realized the deception and flew into the air. They bore down on her, yawping and screeching.

"What do I do? Help me, Zaagi," said Elizabeth, her eyes wide. Her fists tore at the grass surrounding the hole.

"Do exactly as I say. Stand up." Elizabeth nodded and stood up next to the hole. The vultures were closer now. Their cries nearly drowned out Zaagi's instructions.

"Put your hands as far above your head as possible, arms straight." Elizabeth reached her arms to the sky. The vultures careened straight for her, only twenty yards distant. She could see their bloodshot, straw-colored eyes focused on her face. "Close your eyes and jump into the hole," Zaagi said.

Her throat and stomach tightened. *"What?"*

"Do it *now!*" Zaagi yelled as his head disappeared into the dark.

Elizabeth took a deep breath, closed her eyes, and jumped feet-first into the hole. As she fell, the sides of the hole scraped the skin of her arms. She heard the *whoosh* of one of the vultures as it flew over her.

She landed on her backside and hit her head on something

hard and flat. She looked up. Sunlight streamed through the hole above, and she could hear the frustrated screams of the vultures. She shook her head to clear it.

She was in a tunnel, which was about four feet in diameter. She placed her hand against the wall of the tunnel where she had hit her head—it was smooth, like warm clay. Zaagi squatted at her side, peering at her. Bright sparks in the semi-darkness flashed around and above her. She rubbed the back of her head. Her arms ached where they'd scraped along the edges of the hole, and the spot on her lower arm where the vulture had bitten her was swollen purple and dripping blood.

The sparks whizzed by her in both directions and disappeared into the far reaches of the tunnel, as new ones flashed by from the other direction. It made her dizzy even as she tried to ignore them—little flickers of light flying above her head and around her body at lightning speed, barely missing her. *Fireflies?*

Wiping the blood dripping from her arm, her body went cold, and her stomach lurched. A buzzing in her ears grew, and everything around her receded into the far distance. She looked at Zaagi. He stood on his hind quarters and weaved back and forth. Around him spun a halo of yellow fireflies and his eyes were flaming red.

The last thing she remembered before everything went black was Zaagi, who sounded as if he was singing. She remembered the song from somewhere, perhaps a book she had read, and she tried to sing along with him.

At the hole where he went in
Red-Eye called to Wrinkle-Skin.
Hear what little Red-Eye saith:
"Nag, come up and dance with death!"

"Wake up, Elizabeth. This is no time to sleep."

She opened her eyes. Zaagi stared back. His fearsome red eyes were gone. He regarded her with the deep and dark brown eyes she'd known. She relaxed.

"I don't think I was sleeping. I think I fainted. How long…"

"Not long. I fixed your leak."

"My leak?" She looked down at herself. The wound on her arm was still swollen but no longer bleeding and the blood that had dribbled down her forearm was gone.

"Yes. You taste terrible, but I know you'd fix my leak if I had one."

Zaagi had licked her wound to clean it and stopped the bleeding. It was such a personal thing that she blushed. She sat up slowly.

"Thank you. Yes. Of course. I think."

"Who is Nag?"

Elizabeth squinted. The name was from a book that someone had read to her a very long time ago. Beyond that, she couldn't quite place the reference.

"I think a snake, but—I'm not sure." She sighed.

"A snake? I would love a snake right now. My belly is empty."

Elizabeth shivered and rolled her eyes.

"I have to show you something, Elizabeth," Zaagi said.

"Ok, but where are we? What are these tunnels? You couldn't have dug these, could you?" The whizzing fireflies continued to shoot past them from both directions. Zaagi put his paw against the tunnel's side as if he were testing whether it was real or not. He stared at it, then looked back at her.

"No, these are not mine. I don't know if anyone dug them. They've always been here. I think they run through the underside of the whole world."

"And what are these flying sparks?" asked Elizabeth. She grabbed at one of the fireflies with her fist but it easily avoided her grasp.

"You will never catch one, silly girl. I can't catch them and I am much faster than a slow-moving human."

"Hmmm. I think I moved pretty quickly—I kept those stinky vultures from eating you for a snack," she said as she folded her arms.

"For which I am grateful. You did help me save us."

Elizabeth narrowed her eyes. "How about we saved us?"

"No meerkat is an oasis, as was said since ancient times. True."

"I don't know what that means, but I can agree with it. What did you want to show me?"

"This way," Zaagi said and scampered away into the tunnel. Elizabeth tried to stand and hit her head. She hunched over, but that was much too difficult to maintain, so she got down on all fours and began to crawl.

The tunnel, which turned and twisted as they moved forward, was illuminated by the flying sparks and she could see fairly well. The ceiling or roof was smooth but wrinkled, as if water or liquid had once flowed through the tunnel. Zaagi kept stopping and glancing over his shoulder at her.

"I'm crawling as fast as I can," she said. The soft clay of the tunnel floor was easy on her knees and hands. After about half an hour of crawling they came to a fork in the tunnel. Zaagi chose the fork to the right but stopped just as they entered and turned to her.

"Do not get ahead of me. When I stop, you must promise to stop as well."

"I promise," she said. Zaagi nodded and moved forward as Elizabeth followed. As she crawled, she noticed the fireflies were only moving in one direction. They flew from behind them and forward into the new tunnel. None returned the other way. This cut the light in the tunnel by half and made it gloomy. They rounded a small bend and Zaagi stopped. He sat up on his haunches and pointed.

"There."

The tunnel ended in front of them, blocked by a perfectly round disk so black that it seemed to suck in light. The fireflies crashed into it and immolated themselves in little puffs of light and smoke. Only when they met their fate at the surface of the disk did the fact that it even had a surface at all become apparent. Without the tiny explosions, it seemed to be infinitely deep, like the darkest and deepest well she could imagine. She wanted to touch it, to run her fingers over or through the surface. She shuffled forward.

"You promised," Zaagi said. He stood at his full height in front of her. She shook her head. She'd forgotten and couldn't keep her eyes off the black disk.

"I'm sorry. What is it?"

Zaagi stepped back. He moved close to the disk and extended his right paw toward its center. Elizabeth froze.

"Zaagi…"

"Watch."

As his paw entered the disk, there was a hiss and a puff of white smoke curled around his forearm. He held it there for three or four seconds and then pulled it out. The fur on his paw was gone, leaving only gray skin with a reddish-pink hue that stopped at a ring encircling his forearm. He shook it and licked it gently.

"It eats things. I think it eats everything. All of these tunnels are being eaten. They are everywhere now and the tunnels are disappearing," he said. He sighed and sat back on his haunches, staring at her. "My fur will grow back, but if I held it inside much longer, I don't think there would be enough left to grow again. I think my paw would be gone forever."

Elizabeth sat with her back against the curved wall. "You're scaring me," she said. "I don't know where I am, and where I am is being eaten alive." Zaagi moved closer. He put his hairless pink paw on her knee.

"I don't have answers, Elizabeth, but I told you I know where someone is who might help us find your family and your way home, find Bellflower, and perhaps tell us what is happening. We need to move quickly before this…" he turned to look at the disk which was now closer than it was a few minutes ago, "…eats everything and moves to the world above ground."

As the black disk ate its way forward, the walls of the tunnel seemed to convulse—quivering ripples rolled past her and Zaagi.

Elizabeth nodded. "Show me the way. We'll do this together."

Zaagi pointed upward. "That way," he said. Elizabeth got on all fours in the center of the tunnel. Zaagi scampered up her shoulder to her back and began to dig a hole in the ceiling. Dirt fell around them as they dug their way out of the dying tunnel.

CHAPTER FIVE

Words can be delicious

~Elizabeth

After scrambling from the hole, they soon found the path they had been following. The vultures were nowhere in sight. Elizabeth was hungry and Zaagi helped her forage for human food. When she had finished a dinner of dandelions and rutabagas, the last of the day's sunlight began to seep into darkness. They settled beneath a curved arch of brambles and vines near the path that divided a field of hemlocks and walnut trees. A soft breeze brought the scent of lavender and jasmine.

Zaagi munched on a handful of fat, purple beetles he'd uncovered beneath an old rotting log. The fluids ran down his chest and pooled on his belly. Every so often, he scooped up a paw-full and lathered it into his mouth. Elizabeth avoided watching and tried to ignore the crunching noises. Dinner finished, Zaagi dug a shallow burrow and fell asleep inside it almost immediately, but Elizabeth was restless.

She climbed to her feet from beneath the hatch, stretched, and stared at the sky.

"Father? Mother? Where are you? Why am I here alone?" She listened carefully, but all she could hear was the rustling leaves.

Not far away stood a tall hemlock, revealed in the clear light of a full moon. She walked over and sat beneath its outstretched, gnarled limbs. Within the dark tree's shadow, she hugged herself and rocked.

"I don't want to feel sad," she murmured.

"Then what is it you want, child?" asked a deep voice.

Elizabeth jumped and looked up. Not more than twenty feet away sat a coyote, perfectly still except for his twitching tail. He watched her. His yellow eyes gleamed. She scrambled up and pressed her back against the tree trunk.

"My name is Marwolaeth," he said. The sound of the name from his mouth was a sibilant lisp. "But you may call me Coy, for that is what I am."

"I'm not afraid of you," she lied. Hanging out with a meerkat was one thing, but coyotes were calculating and predatory.

Coy shrugged and prowled closer. "Why should you be afraid of me? I mean you no harm. I am not *your* Marwolaeth."

She drew in her breath. "What do you mean?"

"It is an old word: to grant merciful sleep." The coyote's fur shimmered in the moonlight.

Watching Coy, she sat and wrapped her arms around her legs. "Isn't all sleep merciful? What is it you want?"

"Zaagi and I were supposed to have a rendezvous. You

interrupted it. Now you will take him and his heart away from the truth. If you care about him, let him go," said Coy with a low-pitched growl.

"I'm trying to help him," Elizabeth said, and realized this must have been who Zaagi was waiting for when she showed up. She looked at the silver moon through the branches. The leaves rustled in the breeze overhead. Her chest heaved, and she put her chin on her knees. "I need to help him so he can help me find my family. I need to remember who I am."

Coy shrugged. "Why should I care about your troubles?"

"You wouldn't be here talking to me if you didn't want something from me."

Coy glanced at her. "What is your mother's name? Do you have brothers, sisters?"

She looked at her hands and rubbed them, as if the warmth would create a spark. "I can't recall. Today is the only day I remember. When I try to think back, it's like knocking on a locked door."

"You will find what you seek at the center, where all will sleep."

Elizabeth straightened. "The center of what? These woods?"

"At the center," Coy repeated.

"Which center? Where?"

"If I answered, it would only be words. You would hear them, but you wouldn't understand."

"You can tell me, or you can go away. Your choice, coyote," she snapped. She was getting fed up with word games. This whole world seemed to be made up of strangeness and words.

"It's simple. To understand the words, you would have to eat them, so they can become part of you." Coy tipped his head. "Words can be delicious. Or they can be bitter. We taste them, try to savor them, and spit them out."

She looked him over. "Coy is a good name for you. You are shy with the truth and speak in metaphors."

"What is a 'metaphor'?"

"It is when we say one thing is another in order to understand the one thing more deeply."

Coy looked at the sky considering this. "Yes, that is how I speak. Perhaps you are wiser than you look."

"I can't see how you'd help Zaagi. He's an honest creature who speaks his mind, while you conceal everything and speak in riddles."

"If not me, then who?"

"I will help him, as he's helping me." Elizabeth stood and walked from the hemlock shadows. She wanted to put distance between herself and Coy, but she could feel his eyes on her back.

She opened her arms to the pale light and turned in a circle. She couldn't move forward because she didn't know where she was going. She couldn't move backward because she didn't know where she came from. But she had to move so she turned and turned, and the trees waltzed by as if they were dancing. *I would like to dance forever*, she thought.

"The world is the only thing that spins forever." Coy had crept closer without her realizing.

"Did you just read my mind?" Elizabeth asked as she

rotated, the night air warm upon her skin. She watched the coyote as she spun around and around.

"No. But when you understand *my* metaphor, you will find your family," Coy said.

Elizabeth frowned. "Stay away from Zaagi. You may be his Marwolaeth, but he promised to help me find my family. You haven't made any promises, coyote. And those are words you may eat and swallow. Do you understand?"

"I do." Coy backed into the shadows until he disappeared. Elizabeth moved to the arch and laid down beside Zaagi's burrow. His head was visible, and he made little snoring noises.

She placed her hand part way into the burrow on the soft fur of his head and closed her eyes.

Chapter Six

She wrote the way she danced

~Federico

Between visiting Elizabeth each morning and later transcribing my notes, I tried my best to stay busy selling houses, but my mind was not on business.

Meanwhile, I returned to the scene of the crime. I needed a document, a "legal description of property," as they call it, in order to sell the Mulligan home. Carl had moved out after the terrible 'accident' with his wife and was living in a newly purchased mansion. He'd called to notify me that I wouldn't disturb him if I needed to have access to the house or to show it to potential buyers.

"I won't be back so feel free to show the place whenever you want," he'd said over the phone as I stood in the foyer of the empty house.

"I promise I'm doing the best I can. By the way, I heard about the accident. I'm terribly sorry. How is your wife doing?"

There'd been a long silence. "What business is it of yours?" he'd asked. There was another pause as I'd tried to think of a suitable reason to ask about her, but then he spoke again and his tone had softened. "Sorry. I didn't realize you cared. She told me you'd met, but wasn't clear on the details. How well do you know her, exactly?"

"Oh, not well, I'm afraid. We discussed dancing, if I recall. She seemed quite skilled and knowledgeable about it. I know next to nothing, but I do know that *balance* is a key talent."

Another short silence. "I'd like to meet to discuss a few things. 3478 Oak Hills Lane, my new home. Be there around 11:00 a.m. Goodbye." And he'd abruptly hung up.

But that whole conversation was far from my mind as I descended the steps into the darkened basement of the unoccupied house. A single bulb illuminated the stairs. At the bottom there was a switch to turn on the rest of the lights. I turned them on and glanced at the cement floor at the base of the steps. I don't know what I expected to see, perhaps some lingering presence of Marie, some sign of her terrible fate, but there was nothing there. I was relieved and disappointed at the same time.

I rummaged through a file cabinet near the old boiler, looking for the property description. I opened the bottom and last drawer and found a diary with small ballerinas on it. Curious, I opened it. It was Marie's personal journal. She wrote the way she danced, with small, precise loops and whorls, each letter flowing seamlessly yet deliberately into the next.

I closed the book and set it back.

Read it? Close the drawer and walk away? Normally, I wouldn't hesitate to walk away, for it wasn't written for my eyes. But nothing about this situation was normal.

The old boiler kicked on with a *bang*. I could hear once again the music that it made. The decision was easy.

I went back to my car, grabbed my thermos of coffee and my lunch bag, and returned to the boiler room. I pulled a folded lawn chair up, unfolded it under a humming fluorescent light, lifted out the diary, settled in, and began to read.

Chapter Seven

Diary - Tuesday, 9/23/2000

~Marie

Today's my fourteenth birthday. I dreamed last night that I was wandering through a forest. Its green leaves were deep and glistening, and the mossy floor sparkled like crystals. When I looked at the sky, it was bright blue. I was lost and so was the person I'd come to find. I had no idea how to find him or how to get home. I started to cry before I woke up completely.

I rolled over, blinked, rubbed my eyes, and tried to go back to sleep but it was too late. I sat up and looked around to get my bearings. My light blue sheets were warm, but I was shivering. The garbage truck just rattled by. My white carpet needs to be vacuumed but first I need to pick up all the clothes, books, and papers I've left all over the floor. This diary was on my nightstand with a card that said, "Happy Birthday, Marie. Love, Mom and Dad." It wasn't wrapped, and the card was just a business-card-sized piece of cardboard. The daisies and ballerinas on the diary's white cover are nothing I would've picked out for myself. I'm surprised anyone remembered at all though.

Parker, my brother, is missing. He didn't come home after

school yesterday. Mom, school parents, neighbors, and the police are looking everywhere, like the fishing hole in Buck Creek behind the old tannery. That's his favorite place to go.

Two days ago, he tried to talk me into going fishing with him. We have the conversation every week.

"C'mon," he'd said. We were eating breakfast. He ate a huge spoonful of Fruit Loops and smiled while his mouth was full. Milk dribbled down his chin. He has a cleft palate, and he looked gross. Usually, he's self-conscious about his looks, and I'm the one telling him that he's beautiful.

That day, I'd made a face and said, "You're being gross." He laughed at me while I pushed the brown sugar streaks around in my grayish oatmeal, picked up a spoonful, and dumped it back into the bowl. "I'm not touching worms and I'm not going near smelly fish." I'd pushed my bowl away. Everything was gross now.

Now he's gone. I don't think I believe in God. Everyone else seems to be praying for him, but I can't do it.

Dad's gotten worse since the news. He's dying from poisoning from Agent Orange. He fought in Vietnam. It was such a long time ago—before I was born—but I guess sometimes something can get in your blood and poison you a little at a time and you hardly even notice until it's too late.

Mom's even more exhausted than usual. She already works one full-time and two part-time jobs since Dad can't work anymore, and the government has denied responsibility for Dad's being sick. She looks 20 years older than she was yesterday. The tiny wrinkles around her eyes and cheeks got hollow and deep overnight. Dad alternates between yelling at us and crying. And I don't think Mom's sleeping because she's so upset.

I guess that's all I have to say right now.

I feel guilty because I slept okay last night.

Come back, Parker.

Chapter Eight

I'm fishing for a star

~*Elizabeth*

Pale light from the morning sun glazed the field around Elizabeth with a slick sheen. She yawned and stretched. Zaagi still slept under the hatch, snoring and muttering. She tried to ignore him, and circled her hand over a patch of violets beside her. They shivered when her palm brushed the tips of the petals.

She thought about what the coyote had told her. *The center of things.*

She looked up. A bluebird circled high above her. In such a huge sky, that couldn't be an accident. She glanced at the violets reaching for her circling hand.

She decided that she wanted to find the 'center.' Maybe her parents were there, waiting. She gathered herself in her own center and rose like a balloon untethered on a green mist toward the bluebird. *If this is a dream, then I will take control of things.*

The bluebird stopped circling and hung in the sky. It flapped its wings in a blur—a hummingbird-hover—as if waiting for her. Elizabeth merged forms with the bird—her fingers elongated into wingtips, her skin tickled as feathers grew, her eyes tilted to the sides, allowing her to see in a greater arc about her. The bird released its body to her.

After her initial shock began to dissipate, Elizabeth rolled, spun, and dived. Below, she saw her motionless body with Zaagi asleep next to her. At the last second, she pulled up and ascended into the sky, did a barrel roll, and shot away. She skimmed the treetops, buffed the tips of the leaves with her soft, feathery chest. The air became buoyant, full, no longer empty space.

Below her, the meadow and forest give way to a high mesa, barren and rocky except for scattered cottonwood and chokecherry trees. Her heart beat like a drum. She spun and rolled, dove and banked away, playing tag with nothing at all in an ocean of air.

She noticed the goshawk only a second before its talons grasped her back. She twisted away. Quicker, and more nimble than the giant hawk, she pulled her wings tight against her body and dove straight down toward a small pond in a clearing of white birch trees.

Not daring to look behind her, and just feet from the pond's surface, she spread her wings and wrenched her body to the left. The air tore at her wings, nearly ripping them from her body.

A splash came from behind as the hawk crashed into the pond. She shot away, carving a straight line in the pond's calm surface with the tip of one wing, then climbed. Her tiny bluebird heart thundered in her chest. She spun like a corkscrew in the brilliant sun, triumphant.

She returned and relinquished the bluebird's body to its owner. "Thank you," she offered and then sank through the green mist into her own body once again. Above, the bluebird dipped its wings twice and then flew off.

How did I do that? she wondered as she sat up, panting. She felt as if she'd run a marathon.

She glanced at Zaagi, who stirred beside her.

"You're going to cause a lot of trouble around here I can see," he muttered.

Her heart still pounding, she nodded. "You saw me do that? Wow. I wonder if I could do it again. Can you do that, too? How did I do it?"

Zaagi stood, stretched and then rolled in the dust a few times, yawning. "I did, indeed, see it. We have places to go and daylight is never long enough for the business of life." Shaking the dust from his fur, he pointed down the pathway in the direction they had come from. "That way leads to the center of these woods. And that direction," he pointed the other way, "leads to the outside, to the surface of things. There is only one path."

Elizabeth jumped up and looked both ways. "Which way will take us to my family and to Bellflower?"

"I'm not sure, but I told you there's a god that's not too far from here who could help us."

"A *god?* No, you most certainly did not."

Zaagi shrugged. "Well, a demi-god."

"Will this demi-god know why the world is falling apart?"

"We shall find out."

The path that led toward the outside wound through heavy woods. It curved left and right, sloped down, and then up. Although it couldn't be alive, it almost seemed to undulate and toss them into the tall brambles lining both sides. She wondered if it was caused by the black disks consuming the ground they traversed from below.

As they walked, Elizabeth watched Zaagi closely. His thin tail pointed to the sky.

"You're not from here are you Zaagi?"

Zaagi glanced at her and shook his head. "Hardly. This is a horrid place; trees and leaves and grass everywhere. Everything is wet and sticky. How can one see what's happening without long vistas of dry sand and dust?"

"But how did you get here?" Elizabeth asked.

"I woke up here. Just like you did, I suspect."

"With your friend, Bellflower?"

Zaagi's steps faltered for a moment.

"Yes," he said so quietly that she almost didn't hear it. Then he picked up the pace.

The writhing path widened as the trees parted to reveal a clearing exposing a crystal lake. A boy sat on a boulder by the shoreline, a fishing rod in his hand and a wide-brimmed hat over his eyes.

"There he is," Zaagi said.

"Where?" Elizabeth asked, scanning the shore.

"There," insisted Zaagi. "All humans are demi-gods."

"Me too?" asked Elizabeth.

Zaagi nodded. He stood close to her and looked up into her eyes. "You have to be very, very careful, Human Girl."

"Please stop calling me that. My name is Elizabeth. And why do I have to be careful?"

"You can't remember your mistakes."

"Why would I want to remember them?"

"Sometimes meerkats barely survive making a first mistake, let alone a second. You humans may not survive making the same mistake a second time, either. Or someone else may not survive it."

She shifted her gaze to stare at her feet. "You're right. I'm sorry, Zaagi. I'll be careful, I promise." She looked up, but Zaagi was already making his way toward the boy. She hurried to catch up.

"Hello," the boy said as they neared.

"Hello. My name is—"

"Elizabeth. I know."

She was taken aback but asked, "What's your name?"

"Jiibay."

He pushed up his hat revealing his face. He had dark eyes and light brown hair. His skin didn't have a blemish or imperfection and it made her want to turn away, afraid that he'd see all her defects. She could remember a few from her face in the stream. Her nose was too small, and there was a blemish over her right eye, and her chin had a tiny mole near the bottom.

She could see now why Zaagi thought this beautiful boy a demi-god, although she was beginning to doubt if *all* humans were, as she certainly didn't look or feel like a god.

"Hello, Mister Zaagitoon," Jiibay said, looking past her.

"Hello," Zaagi said.

"You are on a journey." Jiibay said. "You are going to find Bellflower and try to free her from her cage. And you are trying to find Elizabeth's family."

"How do you know these things?" asked Elizabeth.

"I can see around time's corner. Just a peek," Jiibay told her with a grin.

Elizabeth found that she couldn't look into those deep brown eyes for long, so instead she looked at his fishing pole. She was surprised to see that the line didn't go into the water but rose into the sky and disappeared into a fluffy white cloud.

"What are you doing?" she asked.

"I'm fishing for a star."

"Why?"

"A good question," said Zaagi. He flicked his ears.

"So its light will let me see all of time," Jiibay said, "instead of just a peek."

"There are no stars during the day," Zaagi said.

Jiibay shrugged. "The sun makes them ashamed. They can never hope to shine as brightly. So, they hide. But they are there just the same."

"How do you catch a star?" asked Elizabeth. "You're just a boy even if Zaagi thinks we're gods. How will you pull it out of the sky?"

Jiibay sat and picked up his fishing pole again. He tugged once to make sure the line was taut. Then he turned and smiled such a brilliant and beautiful smile that Elizabeth blushed. "They're fishing for me," he said. "They'll find me and pull me up when they're ready."

"But I thought you were fishing for *them.*"

"Everything depends on your point of view."

She moved a step closer, intrigued. "Can you see the past?"

"Yes, and the future, but I can only see some of it. I want to see all of it."

"Why would you want to see all of time?" asked Zaagi. "All of time is right now. Time isn't front and back, forward and reverse. It is *boom*, right here."

Jiibay set his pole aside. He held out both hands and opened his fists, palms up, revealing a dove in each one.

"I am the Sun," said the first dove.

"I am the Moon," said the second.

Jiibay looked at Zaagi and said, "You may ask them one question."

"Why me?" asked Zaagi, surprised.

"Because," said Jiibay with a wink, "I can see around the corner that you are the one who will ask the question. I think it is a rare thing to have so many questions in your heart."

Zaagi opened his mouth and then shut it again. He glanced at Elizabeth, then asked, "Where is Elizabeth's family?"

"In my mouth," said the Sun.

"In my tail,'" said the Moon.

Both doves leapt from his hands and flew into the sky, circling round and round each other, and disappeared in the clouds.

Elizabeth shot Zaagi a grateful glance. "Thank you, Zaagi, but you should have asked them where Bellflower is."

Zaagi's nose scrunched and his mouth pursed. "I wasted my question."

Jiibay patted the meerkat's head and smiled. "You gave up your question to help your friend."

"She's not my friend," Zaagi said, but without much ire.

"Then your act of generosity was even greater. You may

ask me your question, Zaagi."

The meerkat sat up excitedly. "Where is Bellflower?"

Jiibay shaded his eyes and scanned the horizon. "Through the Mariposa Valley, across the River Bawaadan, over Mount Beldurra, in a small cage. She rests and dreams of tasty scorpions," said Jiibay.

Then he returned to his fishing pole.

Zaagi danced and jigged around, whooping with joy. Elizabeth laughed to see him so happy but then Jiibay caught her eye. He motioned for Elizabeth to come closer and whispered in her ear, "He will find her, and he will lose her again. But in doing so, his star will find him. There's a star for each of us."

Elizabeth thumped her fist hard against her thigh.

Jiibay reached out and touched her forehead. "If you wish to find your family, go the other direction, toward the center. If you follow your friend to the outside on his quest, they may be lost to you forever." He withdrew his hand and turned to his fishing pole.

"I've had enough riddles," Elizabeth said, scowling. A booming *crack* like thunder shook the lake and surrounding trees, the ground shivered as if a giant boulder had fallen from the sky, and the air around her seemed to glow with the sparkle of a thousand tiny suns.

Zaagi grabbed onto a nearby bush. The thunder quieted,

the sparks dissolved, and the ground became still again.

Elizabeth closed her eyes. She sat next to Zaagi and held her face in her hands, ignoring his stare. "I'm sorry," she whispered, then added loudly, "I don't think I want to be a god. I just want to be a normal person with a family and memories."

Zaagi put his paw on her shoulder, then withdrew it when she didn't respond.

She looked up at the demi-god. "Who am I, Jiibay?"

Jiibay pulled his hat tighter over his head, ignoring her question.

"There are black mouths that will eat this world," Jiibay said as he stared straight ahead and pointed. Elizabeth and Zaagi looked. At the center of the lake, a dark whirlpool spun. Foam and mist danced along its perimeter as the water fell into its center.

"Another black hole, only this time on the surface. What are they?" asked Elizabeth.

"Someone's pain."

"How can we stop them, Jiibay?" asked Zaagi, moving closer.

"If you hurry to the mountain peak, you'll have your answer. You haven't much time."

"Will we succeed?" asked Elizabeth.

Jiibay turned his head to stare at her and Zaagi. "Even the

stars don't know." With that, and with the fishing pole in his hand, he leaned back against his rock and pulled his hat over his eyes.

"Let's go," Zaagi said. "I don't think there are any more answers for us here."

She and Zaagi stood and walked up the path leading from

the lake.

As they crested a small hill, Zaagi glanced back and came to a halt. His eyes bulged. "Look!" He pointed to the trees behind them that circled the lake.

Elizabeth turned. A single star shone, almost as bright as the sun on the other side of the sky. Then Jiibay rose into sight above the treetops, heading toward the star. As he ascended, a brilliant smile shone on his face as both doves circled him. His fishing pole had become a rope of light, which he held in one hand.

Zaagi waved his paw. "Goodbye, Jiibay!"

Jiibay waved back. Then he pointed to his star, before pointing to Elizabeth.

Zaagi looked up at Elizabeth. "What does that mean?"

"There's a star looking for each of us," she said.

A single tear fell down Zaagi's cheek. He wiped it with his paw. "Look what you've done. I'm leaking."

They looked at the sky again, but Jiibay was gone and the bright day-star had faded.

Elizabeth glanced behind them along the path to the center, where Jiibay had told her she'd find her family.

She stared down the path leading to the outside and Bellflower.

She remembered that Zaagi had sacrificed his question to try to help her. There were many things that she couldn't remember, but how important love is wasn't one of them.

"Do you love Bellflower?" she asked Zaagi.

"I don't want to be alive in a world without her. Is that love, Elizabeth?"

She nodded.

Chapter Nine

Diary - 10/06/2000

~Marie

Parker's body was under some old, rusty tin roofs in a pile behind the tannery that I didn't think to look under. When the police came and told us, mom screamed. I've never heard anybody scream like that.

Mom made us macaroni and cheese for dinner while I sat in the living room and stared out the window. Did Parker look like he was asleep when the police found him, or were his eyes open and staring? Mom must have been thinking about him too because after a while the fire alarm screeched and smoke billowed out of the kitchen. I ran in for Mom. She was standing on a chair, waving a newspaper at the alarm on the ceiling.

"Get the pot off the burner," she said.

I picked it up by the handle and put it in the sink. The heat had plastered the macaroni to the bottom and sides of the pot. I ran cold water in it and steam hissed and spread through the kitchen.

"Damnit, Marie! Open a window. Who told you to do that?" Mom yelled.

No one was hungry anyway, I guess. We sat side-by-side on the couch and stared at the blank TV screen. I didn't know if I was supposed to cry or not.

I asked Mom to tell me one of her Ojibwe tribal stories. She has a story for everything. But she just sat there and ignored the question. I watched her out of the corner of my eye and imagined all her stories leaking out of her like her tears. I never thought of Mom as old, but she looked old and tired to me.

She wiped her eyes, went into her bedroom, and returned with a small, framed picture. She handed it to me. I hadn't seen this one before. Dad was in his uniform, smiling, and he was holding Parker who was just a baby. Mom was next to him with her hands on my shoulders. Her hair was pulled back, and she had on a light blue dress with a big, floppy collar. I stood in front of her in a little yellow dress.

"Never let it go. Hang on to it forever," she said. She stood and went back into her bedroom.

I'll never eat macaroni and cheese again.

Chapter Ten

New worlds are born when a god forgets

~Elizabeth

After hours of trekking through the wooded lowlands, Elizabeth was tired, and her feet ached. They walked past rotting logs and swampy ponds covered with a green, stinky film. Overhead, thick, tangled vines hung low in places. They had seen no living creatures since their conversation with Jiibay. It was almost as if all the animals were hiding in fear that something terrible was happening to this world, Elizabeth imagined.

She touched her cheek. Her fingertips stuck to her skin like it was coated with honey. Zaagi's fur was matted from the moisture in the air that clung to both of them, and an acrid, moldy smell invaded their nostrils. They pressed forward along the winding path until, at last, the woods opened out onto a broad and rolling meadow of clover. Gray clouds crossed over the face of the sun. The oppressive humidity retreated, and the air cooled.

The pair stopped at a fallen, moss-covered tree trunk beside the path.

Elizabeth sat down. "I'm exhausted. How far is it to the

outside?"

Zaagi sat beside her, his back curved. He leaned as far back as he could until his feet came up in the air. He wiggled them, causing her to giggle.

"I'm dancing in the air," Zaagi said, then added, "Not farther than one more day."

A yellow butterfly fluttered around her hair before settling on her left shoulder. She nodded at the butterfly. "She's tired too."

A turquoise butterfly landed on the tip of Zaagi's nose. It flexed its wings. His eyes almost crossed as he stared at it. "These are my friends. We are in the Mariposa Valley. That mountain is called Beldurra. It means, 'Mountain of Fear.'"

She looked across the meadow to the red mountain in the distance. A single cloud refused to drift from the edge of the sun and its shadow gripped the mountain like a smoky fist.

"It is where our world ends, and the outside begins." More butterflies appeared, circling, flittering and hovering around them.

"They're so beautiful," said Elizabeth.

Zaagi sighed. "Just so, but they can be annoying little creatures on their own." He shook his foot, upon which five of the creatures had settled, shooing them away.

"On their own?" Elizabeth asked.

An avalanche of butterflies descended. They swirled and

coalesced and dispersed. They formed a giant wheel like the Milky Way. The formation rotated in front of her and Zaagi, rising above them.

Zaagi stood and faced the galaxy of butterflies. He bowed. Elizabeth stood and mimicked him.

"Love and greetings, Memengwaa," said Zaagi. He placed his paw on Elizabeth's leg. "This is my new acquaintance, Elizabeth."

"Love to you, Elizabeth." The voice of Memengwaa was little more than a whisper of air, almost an exhale, created by the simultaneous beating of hundreds of thousands of tiny wings.

"And to you, Memengwaa," said Elizabeth.

"Zaagitoon," whispered Memengwaa, "your Bellflower is well. The human farmer still nurses her to health."

Zaagi stepped forward, clenching his front paws at his side. "She is held in a *cage*. Has the farmer hurt her? Tell me!" Elizabeth flinched at the anger in Zaagi's voice.

"No," Memengwaa said. "As I told you before, her cage is built by love."

"There's no such thing as a cage built by love!" Zaagi stamped his foot.

Memengwaa recoiled. A tendril made of thousands of butterflies extended from Memengwaa's center, the tip inching closer and closer to Elizabeth's forehead. She held still and closed her eyes. The lightest of feathery, fluttering wings brushed her skin. She opened her eyes as the tendril retracted.

Memengwaa's spin slowed and stopped. Butterflies separated and coalesced like a giant mosaic. Elizabeth squinted, and watched the pattern they formed. The insects and the spaces between them became a face, a woman's face: Long hair, soft lips, and a gentle, curved chin.

"It's Elizabeth!" Zaagi exclaimed

"No," whispered Memengwaa.

"Mother." The word flittered from Elizabeth's mouth like a butterfly. "It's my Mom." She could smell fried bread and smoked salmon. The scent made her throat tighten and her nostrils tingle.

Home, she thought, and fought back a tear.

The face burst into a giant swirl of butterflies, and Memengwaa began her spin again.

"How do you know her?" Elizabeth asked. She wiped her eye with the sleeve of her shirt.

"I understand pieces. You are shattered. You must come together," said Memengwaa.

"Where are my pieces, Memengwaa?"

"Look around you. New worlds are born when a god forgets."

"Do you mean this world? I've forgotten almost everything. Can you help me remember?"

Memengwaa spun faster.

"Where fire burns an ancient forest, a new forest grows. Anything can become a seed in the rebirth of memory."

"How? What should I do? I'm so tired."

"Release your grip. When you tire on your long journey and darkness closes around you, lie back in my arms and, like the sea, I will hold you. Look up at the stars as you float on my love, and they will sing to you."

Memengwaa rose into the sky.

Elizabeth and Zaagi stood close to each other. The galaxy that was Memengwaa came apart, and the ocean of butterflies dispersed. Elizabeth held her face in her hands. A sea of butterflies had spoken to her and shown her an image of her mother. She looked at Zaagi.

He reached his paws toward her. She picked him up and he snuggled into her shoulder. She wrapped her arms around him and held him tight, then sat against the fallen log. His fur was as soft as down and she could feel his heart beating. They fell asleep in each other's arms.

Chapter Eleven

The Twelve-Petaled Rose

~Federico

I sat opposite Carl Mulligan, who lounged in his wingback chair, his trousers pressed so crisply I could still see the crease. He sipped Chivas Regal and dangled a loafer on his sockless foot.

Green curtains framed tall windows. Beyond, the land dipped slowly toward a lake, a few apple trees between where the autumn sun's reflection glinted like flakes of foil on a blue mirror. His den was ultra-masculine—claret-colored leather couch and chair, mahogany desk and bookcases, a gigantic flat-screen TV. The only glaring exception was a full-sized portrait of Marie that hung above the fireplace's mantle. It was breathtaking. Lavender blue wisteria flowers cascaded on both sides of her like a waterfall. She wore a full-length, white satin dress, her body turned to the left as if she was about to leave, and her face glanced back over her shoulder to look directly in your eyes. She was smiling slightly, almost as if she were about to ask you to follow her, or to say goodbye, perhaps.

"Why haven't you sold my house yet, Mr. Garcia?"

"Please, call me Federico. The market's depressed, as you

know, Mr. Mulligan," I said with what pleasantness I could muster.

Mulligan had made a fortune buying most of Mount Pleasant prime real estate, including the lumber yards that employed most families in a thirty-mile radius. If anyone could be said to own a town, Mulligan owned ours.

"Mr. Garcia," he said. He set his drink down and picked up a dark, rolled cigar and began to wet the end. "Your clients are mostly low-income buyers with poor or no credit, correct?"

I knew very well the reason Carl had hired me. I was cheap. My fees and commission were the lowest in the county as I struggled to build a clientele. My mouth was dry. Mulligan hadn't offered me as much as a glass of water. I sat uncomfortably in a straight-back chair. "True." I smiled. "In this market, a buyer is a buyer, as you're well aware."

He snorted. "I have yet to see a buyer."

"If you're unhappy with the work I'm doing, there are plenty of other agents in town. I'd actually prefer to discuss something else." I shifted in my chair. I kept my expression as neutral as I could and did my best to maintain eye-contact.

A grimace twisted his lips as he looked away. He lit his cigar and exhaled clouds of gray smoke. "You want to talk about Marie."

I nodded. He waved his cigar back and forth, clearing the smoke from the air between us.

I looked past Mulligan to the lake through the windows. Sweat broke out on my forehead, despite the brutal air conditioning in Mulligan's new million-dollar mansion.

"She and I are friends. Things don't add up, Mr. Mulligan."

His mouth curled into a caricature of a smile. "I suspected as much." He reached for his glass of scotch and put his cigar out in it. He leaned forward and began to pick lint from his trousers.

"Listen to me," he said. His voice had dropped a register, but his posture was relaxed. "I love Marie and she loves me. When I met her, she was so much like a child—a sweet, innocent, perfect child. You've felt the need to protect, haven't you? To harbor and shield? I've kept her safe, given her a haven from the ugly things and the vile people in this world. I don't know what she told you. I don't care. She's happy with me, she knows what I've sacrificed to give her everything she could ever want."

I coughed loudly and raised an eyebrow. He glanced briefly at me and continued.

"*She's* the one who prefers to stay home, who chose her life here with me. She knew who I was—she knows who I am." His voice rose. "I don't recall seeing you around for the last five years. What do you know about her? You know nothing about her. In fact, I don't want you around her ever again."

His eyes stared at the portrait of Marie and then flashed

back to me. He gripped the arm of his chair until his fists turned white. "I have a golfing friend waiting for me. Maybe you know him? Daniel Carrington."

I knew Carrington all right. He was a corrupt State Regulator who oversaw licensing of real estate agents. Mulligan was issuing a not-so-veiled threat. On the lake through the window, I watched a small family of ducks scatter when a swan burst into their midst. Wings flapping and spraying water, the flock split up in every direction. I could have sworn it was one of Elizabeth's swans. The ducks re-formed at the edge of tall reeds near the shore. The swan dipped its head and circled in the crisp brilliance, the curve in its long neck forming a question mark. I looked back at Mulligan, whose eyes were hooded and ominous.

"Ah yes, a prompt tee-off is always important. I won't keep you. And I'm sure Marie won't mind."

He froze.

"How dare you," he said. His eyes flashed. "A half-rate spic with a chip on your…"

"You pushed her, didn't you?" I said quietly. My voice was as solid as granite. He flinched. His face twisted into a snarl. He opened his mouth to say something, seemed to think better of it and let out a deep breath. His snarl turned to a sneer.

"Don't ever presume to talk to me about my wife. Don't ever presume to talk to me or her again. You're fired. Now get the hell out of here."

Now that I knew that he'd tried to hurt her by refusing to deny it, I noticed the swan was gone. I felt the hurt, raging man inside of me kick down the door I'd struggled to keep him behind. A single cloud seized the sun with a thick-veined fist for a few brief seconds. But that was enough.

I stood and regarded the man before me. He was a short man in too-expensive clothes, sitting in a lounge chair, spouting veiled threats and ethnic slurs. My body went from hot to cold as my fists clenched.

I took a step forward, and Mulligan flinched. I grabbed the half-empty bottle of Chivas and walked to the bar. I poured three fingers into a brandy snifter, downed half, and returned to stand behind him.

"I told you to get out of here." His voice wavered.

I grabbed a fistful of his hair, which was stiff from hairspray, and yanked his head backwards. His mouth dropped open and his pupils widened. He tried to swing at me from behind but his fists struck nothing but air.

I saw his lips move into a word that looked like 'please,' but the scotch and a ringing noise filled my head. My voice was liquid mercury—cold, mellow, and dangerous. I didn't recognize it. "Tell the truth, Carl. Tell me the truth. If you do, I'll leave and you'll never see me again."

He struggled and twisted, but my grip on his hair was tight.

With one hand, I lifted him partly out of his chair by his hair as I downed the rest of the scotch with the other. He screamed as his fists flailed, a few connecting with my chest and arms but they hardly registered to me.

There was a muffled groan. I set him back into the chair as he began to sob. A bit of blood trickled down onto his ear where a small clump of hair had been torn out.

"It was an accident. I didn't mean for her to fall. I swear I didn't know she was so close to the edge." I nodded and released his scalp.

As I left, he was curled in his stuffed leather chair. He wouldn't look at me. He buried his face in his hands and shook as he wept. His spine rose and fell in short jerks.

"I'll never let her go. She loves me and she always will." I barely caught his words, being half way out of the room.

I tossed the snifter to the floor where it clattered and rolled under a sofa.

When I got home it was nearly dusk. I'd stopped for a few beers. My shoulders ached, and I was still in the grip of my fugue. I couldn't transcribe my notes from Elizabeth. Instead, I went to the basement and started to lift weights. I watched the rose on the inside of my left arm glisten under a sheen of sweat and pulse with each curl of the dumbbell. Twelve petals. One for each Afghan soldier I'd been ordered to plow into the dust of Babylon while still alive, with an earth-moving vehicle.

I dropped the weight, moved to the concrete wall and smashed my fist against it. The pain ebbed to a dull, stinging throb. My arm was dead weight. I rested my other hand on the wall and leaned forward as I panted. Sweat rolled down my face and past the bridge of my nose. I watched small drops fall to the floor. When my breathing slowed, I wrapped my bloody fist in a towel and collapsed on the cement floor.

I'd probably made things worse for Marie.

Upstairs in the kitchen, I threw the towel in the sink, avoided looking at my throbbing hand, and rewrapped it. I went out the back door and sat on the porch. There were no trees in this wasteland, the town's low-rent district. The power poles across the street thrummed, and a wine-colored sun winked out just above the Mulligan Saw Mills in the distance.

I wanted to talk to Marie. I wanted to reach out and dance with her. My empty arms ached for her embrace.

I gazed at the sky as the first stars appeared. I imagined each one was a candle in a window, inviting me home.

Chapter Twelve

Release your grip, and you will live

~Elizabeth

Deep orange streaks of sunlight swept the Mariposa Valley as the sun rose. Blue-black clouds scudded across the sky as though they were trying to swallow the sun.

Zaagi climbed from his burrow and stretched. He sat up and looked at Elizabeth, who was also sitting.

"Did you sleep well, Zaagi?"

"So I did." Zaagi stood and surveyed the valley. He pointed. "That way is Mount Beldurra. Our world ends at the peak of the mountain, which we must climb. The path to the mountain also crosses a river called Bawaadan. The current is rapid and deep with sharp rocks along its base."

"So, it's very dangerous?"

"Yes. It is said you will forget everything if you fall into the river, assuming you don't drown."

She placed her hand on his shoulder. "Then we'll protect each other. If I fall, you'll catch me and if you fall, I'll catch you. I can't afford to lose more memories."

The two headed along the path toward the crimson

mountain. As they walked, the last of the orange glow died away to be replaced with thin, wispy clouds lacing through a pale blue sky. Elizabeth squinted at something near the skyline.

"What's that?" she asked, pointing. Zaagi looked briefly, then hopped up and down.

"I can't see a thing except trees," he said.

Elizabeth reached for him. "May I?"

Zaagi sighed. "Fine, but it better be worth risking a broken neck." He stepped closer and raised his paws. She picked him up and set him on her shoulder. Holding him steady with one hand, she pointed at a small black circle near the horizon. Another black hole, only this time in the sky.

Zaagi squinted. "Yes, I see it. Now put me down before you drop me. Heights are for birds," he glanced at her, "and human girls."

She set him back on the ground.

"We need to get going, Zaagi."

"I think you're right." The two hurried forward down the path.

In early afternoon, they came to the foot of Mount Beldurra. The River Bawaadan roared and blocked the path to the mountain. The rushing current screamed and howled as it smashed against boulders. Elizabeth's ears popped from the noise.

A straight and narrow log ran from one bank across the

river, which flowed through a small canyon below, to the other

side. It appeared to be the only means of crossing. As she and Zaagi drew closer, Elizabeth noted that the log didn't look particularly sturdy. The bark on the top had been worn away through many years of foot and paw traffic. It looked like it could hold Zaagi's weight, but not that of a fourteen-year-old girl. Worst of all, it was covered with a slippery-looking sheen.

"We're crossing on *that?*" Elizabeth yelled to Zaagi above

the noise from the river.

"Stay close behind me and do as I do," he shouted back.

She nodded and gave Zaagi a thumbs-up. Zaagi stuck his paw out in imitation. Elizabeth giggled and bumped his paw with her fist.

They carefully approached the log. The mist coated Zaagi's fur and made Elizabeth's hair cling to her forehead. She wiped her damp hands on her jeans, knelt, and crawled onto the end of the log on her hands and knees.

Zaagi walked a third of the length of the log, then stopped. He looked back at her over his shoulder and motioned for her to follow. Elizabeth frowned and yelled, "I'm coming!"

She crawled along the wet log and refused to look down, but the river's roaring noise made it difficult to concentrate. She looked at Zaagi, who nodded, then turned again and hopped forward a few feet more.

Elizabeth inched along, staring at her hands. She grasped the log and scooted, each time barely letting her fingers leave the slippery bark.

Zaagi gave her a wave and smiled. His hind legs shot out on the slippery log, as if he were running. He was falling.

Elizabeth stood, pointed her toes and shuffled forward as fast as she could manage.

Zaagi kicked his hind feet to regain control, and his front paws spun in the air. His feet shot out from under him.

In one quick motion, she launched herself forward. She landed on her stomach. It knocked the wind out of her body with an *oomph*. Her legs wrapped around the log. She reached with her right hand and grabbed his hind leg. She squirmed from a sharp pain in her sternum.

Zaagi's weight swung out over the log toward the water, and it spun her around until she was hanging upside down, one arm around the log, Zaagi swinging from the other. They dangled, swaying in the breeze and mist.

"Don't let me go!" he screamed.

She closed her eyes and tightened her grip around Zaagi's ankle. Water squished between her fingers from his fur. Her arm loosened by a fraction and the two of them dropped closer to the water. Opening her eyes, she saw that the far bank was only a few feet away. The roar of the river faded as she focused on their destination. There was nothing but soft grass, no rocks or trees.

She swung Zaagi back and forth. Stabbing pain burst through her shoulder. She sucked in her abdomen and pinched her lips so she wouldn't cry out. Zaagi, it appeared, figured out her plan. He shifted his weight with each swing to help her. With all her strength, she twisted her body and swung him over her head, releasing his foot.

Zaagi tumbled through the air and landed with a muffled *thump* on the near bank, with several feet to spare.

The force of the toss ripped the log from the crook of her left arm. Her upper body swung down. Her arm ached and she sucked in her breath and tightened her ankles' grip as she hung upside down above the current.

She shivered. Her soaked jeans weighed her down. Her shoulder throbbed and her ankles began to numb.

Elizabeth took a deep breath. She clenched her abdominal muscles and exhaled as she forced her torso up, a few inches toward the log. Her chest tightened and her stomach cramped. Her fingers brushed the log before she fell again. She allowed herself to hang there. She was going to drown, not even knowing who she was.

A weight settled on her ankles, and she looked up. It was Zaagi. He hugged her ankles together. He screamed something, but all she heard was the river's roar.

She shivered and her teeth chattered. White foam on the river's surface flashed by below. Her ankles slipped and she dropped a few inches. This was the end.

A man's voice she recognized boomed in her mind from behind her locked door, "A warrior is born in your heart."

I won't panic, Father, she thought, her teeth clenched.

She looked up. Zaagi, it seemed, was perfectly willing to panic. He flailed his arms. "Hold on! Hold on, unsquashable girl! She's coming!" He pointed behind her, but her head was an unmovable anchor pointed toward the river. She closed her eyes and fought to keep her ankles together.

She imagined her mother's long black hair and hazel eyes and thought she heard her speak. "Never let it go. Hang on to it forever." She handed a framed picture to Elizabeth. There was a man, a woman, and two children in it.

Something tickled Elizabeth's chin. Then both her ears at once.

She opened her eyes, dizzied by the movement all around her.

Hundreds, thousands, millions of butterflies swarmed so thick around her that she could hardly breathe. A voice whispered, "Release your grip, and you will live. Lie back, and I will hold you."

Elizabeth placed both hands across her chest, closed her eyes, and let her aching legs relax. She fell only a short distance before landing on a pillow of butterflies. Her body sank towards the river as the butterflies struggled to support her weight. The river flowed with color as thousands of tiny bodies drowned beneath her, crushed by her weight, swept deep down and away by the whirlpools. Yet still they came from every direction to support her body. They fought gravity and the raging torrent to lift her.

"Memengwaa! You're falling apart!" Elizabeth yelled.

"I will be born again by the chrysalis of time. But you are coming together," Memengwaa whispered.

Elizabeth rose just above the lip of the bank. The last few hundreds of thousands that had once made up Memengwaa, exhausted and dying, laid her on the edge of the river bank. Those few who were left alive dispersed, carried away on a brief northern breeze like milkweed seeds to the far corners.

The last thing Elizabeth remembered was Zaagi sitting on her chest, tears in his eyes, rubbing his nose against hers before darkness closed in on her.

Chapter Thirteen

Too much in the world to remember and know

~Elizabeth

With her eyes closed, Elizabeth heard rain in the distance. She knew she'd slept but had no idea how long. The rumble of far-away thunder rolled over her. It was the kind of thunder that made her want to snuggle deeper into covers. It brought her more comfort than worry and made her glad she was alive.

A memory tugged at the corner of her mind. She examined the fragment: the edge of a white pillow with someone's long brown hair draped over it and the corner of an open window, some feet beyond from which a lemon-yellow curtain billowed.

She took the fragment and placed it on a blank canvas on an easel in her mind. She conjured a painter's palette and brush, but on the palette were not just colors but sounds, textures, smells and tastes.

She began to piece herself together. She painted her mother onto the fragment of the white pillow, asleep, then painted herself. She added the thunder and the rain to complement her mother's rhythmic breathing.

She combined the smells of a fresh spring rain with a sweet and faint lilac fragrance on her mother's skin. She mixed the feel of sleek, creamy linens with the weight of a fluffy comforter on her curled body.

She lay for a long time beside her mother and gazed on her sleeping face, content.

Something tickled her chin. Little paws? She heard a squeak, and twitched her mouth. With a great effort, she opened her eyes.

A chipmunk with sable fur stared at her. Its tiny front paws rested on her lips. Tilting its head to the side, it shot away like an arrow. Elizabeth jerked, startled.

Soft ferns fell off her like a blanket as she sat up. Zaagi had covered her as she slept. She looked around. She was in a cave.

Shifting her weight, she winced at a sharp pain in her shoulder. She rubbed it, careful not to apply much pressure.

"Zaagi? Where are you?" her voice echoed.

Thunder cracked. She looked toward the cave's mouth which was at the top of a long pathway of sand. She blinked to focus in the dim light.

Clumps of glowing indigo moss covered the entire roof of the cave. Thousands of tiny crystals twinkled like stars among the dim blue glow.

Something in her periphery moved. A large boulder rested against the cave wall about twenty feet from her and on the top, the chipmunk watched her. In the time it took Elizabeth to get unsteadily to her feet, it had gone.

Then the creature was there again, flitting left and right, almost too quick for her eyes to focus.

"Stop it!" she yelled.

The chipmunk stopped. It sat on the boulder and stared.

"My name's Elizabeth. I'm sorry, I didn't mean to yell at you. Who are you, Mr. Chipmunk?"

"My name's Jamu, pleased to meet you." Jamu's voice rang like a quartz chime. "And I'm a girl, just like you."

"Really? A girl? And have you seen a meerkat, Jamu?"

"Today, he went thataway," she chimed. As she spoke, her tail flicked over her head and jabbed toward the opening of the cave. "Along with the tricky one, too: rascally wicked, forever adieu!"

"You mean a coyote?" Elizabeth's heart dropped. Marwolaeth. *If you hurt him, I will hunt you down and—*

"I do, I do! But Zaagi left some words for you."

"He left me words?"

Jamu nodded. "In me. Everything, I remember forever— whatever, whenever, whoever." She sighed. "Sometimes too much for a chipmunk to tell and show, too much in the world to remember and know."

Elizabeth moved closer to the boulder and sat. She smiled at Jamu.

"It beats not being able to remember or know anything at all," she said. She shook her head and glanced at her palms.

Jamu scampered from the boulder to sit in front of Elizabeth.

"I know what to do, troubled girl so blue. Travelers come from all over the world, pass here, and tell their joy, their love and their woe." She pointed to the glittering moss, and added, "Each one a story, each one is true. I'll tell you what of yours I've heard and know."

Elizabeth stared at Jamu and shook her head. "But Zaagi… I don't have time for stories. He'll blame himself for what happened to Memengwaa. Will you tell me what he said?" Elizabeth scuffed her foot against the cave's floor. "Memengwaa's gone, and it's all my fault."

"I will. But first trust me. You will see." Jamu scurried up the incline leading to the outside.

Elizabeth rose and followed Jamu's tiny footprints in the sand. She climbed toward the oval opening to the cave. Jamu's outline was dark against the gray and dreary landscape outside the cave. The wind whipped the rain in gusts, occasionally driving it almost horizontally as thunder roared. Jamu sat at the lip, her back to Elizabeth, and watched the violent storm. Elizabeth sat beside the chipmunk and took a deep breath.

"Where are we?"

Jamu looked at her and back at the outside. "Gichi Manidoo."

"What strange words," she said, then stopped. She

frowned. "No, wait. They sound familiar… What do they mean?"

"Gichi Manidoo? Why, they belong to *you*."

Elizabeth sighed. *Why does everyone in this place talk in riddles?* "Tell me what you mean, Jamu. Please."

Jamu turned to look at Elizabeth, her whiskers twitching.

"They're your mother's words, now yours, you see? It means 'Great Spirit.' Her proud Ojibwe people live and speak, their blood runs red and true, through her, in you. I see them in your eyes, your face."

"And where is Gichi Manidoo?"

Jamu scurried into the cave, a tiny rooster-tail of sand spraying behind her churning paws. Elizabeth shook her head, turned, and followed her.

"It's a story, a story we tell ourselves in order to be free." Jamu turned and pointed at the thousands of flashing points of light in the indigo moss. "Each light is a story, you see."

Except for the continuous sound of the distant rain and thunder, the main cavern was silent. Jamu had disappeared as Elizabeth stared at the twinkling stars in the moss. She checked behind the boulder. Jamu wasn't there, but she found a giant pile of peanuts beside another pile of empty shells. She reached for one and grasped the peanut between her fingers, but before she could raise her arm, a fuzzy flash grabbed it away and disappeared. As she stepped back, Jamu appeared with the peanut on the top of the boulder and held it out to her.

"Would you like a peanut, dear? You have no manners, it's clear."

Elizabeth's cheeks flamed. "Oh, goodness. How rude of me. I would love a peanut, thank you." She took the peanut, cracked the shell and ate it. It was crunchy and sweet. She was about to drop the empty shell on the ground but Jamu watched her through narrowed eyes. Elizabeth placed the empty shell on the pile behind the boulder.

Such a tiny gift as a peanut made her feel a deep longing for home. She'd kept it in check, but now it overpowered her. She felt a thump on her thigh and looked down. She struck her fist repeatedly against her leg. She couldn't stop doing it. Pressure rose from her belly and spread through her chest, tightened around her heart and made it ache. She turned her back to Jamu, and her shoulders shook. She slumped forward and wept until the heaving gasps from her chest subsided and her breathing calmed.

She wiped her tears with the back of her hand, relieved that at least the pressure was gone, for now. She looked up at the twinkling diamonds in the ceiling. "Tell me one of the stories, Jamu," Elizabeth said. Jamu also looked up and, just above her, one of the diamonds glowed brighter and brighter.

Elizabeth sat down, rested her chin on her hands and waited.

"I will tell you an amazing story, exactly as it was told to me."

Chapter Fourteen

Diary - 10/08/2000

~Marie

Dad died yesterday evening, and now it's just me and Mom. My father and brother will be buried at the same time and place. Half of the people I've always known are gone. Mom reminded me, it only takes two people to make a family.

Yesterday, I helped prop Dad on his pillows and sat with him. Mom's dreamcatcher from Grandma Aki hung over the headboard. It's the size of a baseball, and its webbing is smooth, framed by curved sticks woven around each other in an intricate web. Feathers hang from the bottom by stiff, braided horsehair. When Parker and I were small, Mom would hang it over our heads at bedtime. I remember watching it spin as she held it way up. The feathers seemed to stretch toward our faces as my eyes closed. Mom had hung it over Dad's bed. He didn't want it there, but he didn't argue with her.

I'd curled up next to Dad. He'd opened his mouth, took a breath, and had said, "Marie." He'd coughed so hard that he shook and sweated, and blood had spattered on his shirt. "I'm going to heal from this, you wait. And when I do, I'll show you how to be a warrior."

I wished I hadn't argued with him. I didn't know then it would be our last conversation. "Maybe I don't want to be a warrior. You told Parker that he was a warrior, but you never told me that I was until today, now that he's dead," I'd said.

He took a deep, shuddery breath, and his eyes got soft and wet.

I turned from him and I hit my leg hard, a few times. Lately, I like pain. I mean it doesn't feel good, but it feels real. It isn't the nice words people say to you about pain at a funeral; it's right there. I didn't want him to see me do it, though.

"A warrior isn't a boy or a girl. A warrior is born in the heart first," he'd said.

"Will you teach me?" I asked.

"I just said I would, darling."

I kissed his forehead and climbed out of his bed to leave him to rest. As I put my hand on the doorknob, he'd said, "Tell me the truth rule."

I looked at him and rolled my eyes. He waited for an answer and I had no choice but to say the words. "Always tell the truth, but only truths that don't hurt people."

He smiled, and his cheeks were wet with tears. A memory flashed—me as a little kid, tripping in the tight, shiny shoes I had to wear for company one Easter. I'd stumbled into the kitchen and he whipped around and caught me in his arms, swung me over his shoulder, and kissed my cheek before setting me down.

"Go wash the dishes," he said. "Don't give your mom one more thing to do than she already has to."

The kitchen was already pretty clean, but my blue-flowered plate, with its mustard smears and bread crusts was still on the table along with the mostly-drunk bottle of pop. I brought them to the sink, dumped the rest of the bottle, and held the plate as I stood and looked out the window.

The tears came hard and fast. I left the plate in the sink and ran. I barely made it to my bedroom before the crying made it too hard to see where I was going. I slammed the door and flopped on my unmade bed, with its girly unicorn sheets and pink, too-puffy comforter. It's a little kid's room. I'm not a little kid anymore, Parker's dead, and I know Dad won't be teaching me anything. My childhood feels far away, like it's happening to someone else.

I buried my face in my pillow, and sobbed into its dumb, pale blue unicorn face. I cried for Parker, and for Dad, and for Mom. But I can't cry for myself. I can be honest and cry for others, but my own truth, my own losses—I can't even name them in my head. It hurts too much.

From now on, I'm going to be careful what truths I tell myself.

Chapter Fifteen

The profanity of the darkness

~Federico

We were in a hole in the Afghanistan Mountains. Me, Shane Budowski and Lou Barker. Pinned down.

I knew Budowski was screwed when I pushed the torn shreds of his large intestine back into the gaping hole just above his left hip. The sepsis would kill him, as would the lost blood soaking the dirt we squatted in. Lou kept gagging and looking away, then looking back again. The moon was a spotlight, and I couldn't avoid looking at the wound anymore, either, so I decided I'd just tuck them back in. His guts ballooned back out every few minutes, and so I gave up.

"Kill the horse, kill the horse!" Budowski shouted, obviously delirious.

Lou moaned in frustration, "What is he talking about?" I shrugged, and he half-whispered, "Shut up, Ski. Ok? Please, bro, shut the hell up."

I laid back and looked up through the tangled branches of a giant cypress tree that hung over our hole, Budowski's head in my lap. The heat was a sweaty hand over our mouths. I was hoping the Taliban had gotten tired of messing with us and left, but they would probably be back soon. A fat spider, like a walking pustule, yellow with green spots on its back, scuttled across my arm, down my leg and onto my useless M-16—no revulsion or concern, not even curiosity. Some platoon leader I was, with not even the strength or initiative to brush the bastard off.

Lou's arm was twisted in the sling I'd made from Ski's shirt, and he couldn't see from his left eye, now swollen like a ripe plum. I could barely hobble on my right foot, gangrene-laced from the rusty ten-inch nail carefully placed for some dumbass like me to step on—no doubt wiped in goat shit or something.

I gently shifted Budowski, then crawled to rummage in Lou's medic-kit. I pulled out the last three morphine syringes.

"I wanna die, oh Jesus, I wanna die..." Budowski babbled.

The pain in my foot was excruciating; like a dull knife being slowly pushed through the top, then withdrawn, then pushed in again. Lou watched me take the syringes out. His teeth chattered. He spat in disgust when I moved to Budowski with all three in my hand.

"You're wasting them," he said, and looked the other way. I hoped they would put Budowski over the edge. His skin was white, blood dribbling down his chin.

I was putting one to his thigh when I glanced over the lip of our depression and saw the horse—a magnificent, pure white mare, outlined against a ruby flame of mountain rock, a few hundred yards from us. She seemed so natural, so right—she belonged deep in the Afghan wilderness as much as we did, although the utter strangeness of its existence in this place barely registered in my mind.

"My God. Do you see that?" Lou wheezed.

"Yeah. Glad you do, too."

The mare watched us warily while grazing on some sparse vegetation. Lou slid over, and placed his good hand on the side of Ski's throat.

"Adios, bro," he said a few seconds later. I barely noticed Ski's death, I was so fascinated by the horse. Maybe it escaped from a circus, I mused.

From above came the wump-wump-wump of an incoming friendly Chinook. Lou tottered up and pulled me to my feet. I tried to grab hold of Budowski, but Lou yanked me up and out of our hole. I shook my head and jumped back in, groaning from the pain in my foot. Lou swore up a storm but joined me again and we wrestled Budowski's body up and out.

As we half-careened and stumbled toward the noise, carrying the corpse, the unmistakable clatter of the helicopter's M-240B broke out and I watched, like a slow-motion Sam Peckinpah movie, as the horse was cut into bloody pieces. I knew someone had decided to have some fun and I started yelling through the din at the now visible chopper, but I don't remember what I said. It was too late for the horse, anyway.

The chopper dipped when they saw us and headed our way. It settled in a narrow opening between giant boulders, and they pulled us on. We lifted off as gunfire broke out a few thousand yards to the south.

"Did you see that goddamn horse?" the gunman yelled and slapped his thigh repeatedly. "That was sweet!" The last thing I remember before passing out were the tracers, still visible in the early dawn mist, pounding what was left, making bone and flesh jump like wet sawdust on a drum.

Lou and I talked only once after we were medevacked out. I'd done one more tour in Afghanistan and then, a few years later, we met at the Vietnam Memorial in Washington. He swears the horse was some kind of guardian angel, who sacrificed itself for us, protected us. I know better—she wasn't an angel *or* demon.

I'd thought he was crazy, but I know what Budowski meant now. I'm almost glad (almost) that someone had killed that magnificent animal. There are places and times that beauty and grace don't belong. Better to snuff the light ourselves, sometimes, than to let the sublime be sullied by the profanity of the darkness.

Chapter Sixteen

Jamu Tells the Story of the Stranger

~Elizabeth

Long ago, when humans lived peacefully and in harmony with the land, there was a village near a vast lake called Gitchigumi. One autumn, a storm took the lives of most of the men in the village while they were fishing. The following summer, an old man came to them, a stranger from far away. He carried nothing but the clothes upon his back and a knife at his hip. He also carried the memories, in the scars upon his body, of many battles fought during his long life as a warrior. His hair was silver, tied in a ponytail, and his eyes were a clear and piercing green.

The women offered him food and drink. "Why have you come here?" asked one.

"I am tired and near the end of my journey," he said. Mellow and rich, his voice rolled like the slow waves of Gitchigumi in the summer morning.

"You are welcome to our food, but you cannot stay," said another. "You are a stranger. Why don't you return to your own village to finish your journey?"

"This is my home. I am a son, a brother and a father to all of you. I have returned at last from a mission to avenge you, a mission which you sent me on long ago. This I have done."

At this, they were astonished. None recognized him or remembered him.

"Perhaps that is so and perhaps it is not, but even if true, that was many years ago," said an old woman with long white hair and a necklace of topaz who was the Village Elder. "Rest here, then return to your journey. Son or not, you no longer belong to us."

"You may stay in my shelter as long as you like," said a young maiden, stepping forward. Her name was Aiyana, and although she was short, her back was as straight as an arrow's shaft, and her face was open. She turned to the villagers and added, "My mother died long ago giving me life, and my father died one year gone upon the Gitchigumi with your fathers, sons and husbands. I am an only child, and I know loneliness. This gentle man claims kinship. I am ashamed of all of you."

Hakan, one of the few young men who had not been on the fateful fishing trip, also stepped forward. "Aiyana. You don't know this man. *We* don't know this man. It is not proper or right for you to make such an offer. Let him find his way to some other village."

To the Stranger, he said, "Go now. You are not welcome here." He folded his arms and glared at the Stranger, at whom all in the village were now looking.

"Hakan, mind your manners," said Aiyana.

Hakan glanced at her, shifted his weight, but remained steadfast.

The Stranger smiled at Aiyana, then nodded to Hakan.

"Thank you. But I will build my own shelter some distance down the coast, near enough to be of help if you should need me, but far enough so as not to disturb any of you."

"What help could we need from an old wanderer with nothing to show but dusty clothes on his back?" asked Hakan. He turned on his heel and walked away.

Aiyana sighed, then stepped close to the Stranger. "I am sorry for Hakan. He knows better. Please reconsider my offer?"

The Stranger shook his head. "He is right, it would not be proper."

"Thank you for the food and drink," he said, addressing everyone now. "It is more than I could have hoped for."

He turned to leave, but Aiyana touched his arm. He stopped and turned back. She opened her mouth to speak but could not remember what she wanted to say. His eyes were gray like the winter wolf but tinged with the emerald hues of a vast sea.

"He will be trouble if you are not careful," the Stranger said quietly, so only she could hear.

Aiyana blinked, then frowned. "Hakan? He is no trouble."

The Stranger gave a gentle smile. "Farewell, Aiyana. You are a courageous and kind soul."

"Wait! What is your name?" Aiyana called as he walked away, but he did not turn back or answer.

The Stranger followed the coast until the village was no longer in sight. He climbed a high dune to a cliff overlooking the great lake. Near its edge, he built a small but sturdy shelter. Surrounded by white birch trees and blue spruce, he gathered wood for a fire, then bathed in the lake's cold, clear water. In the evening, he slept beneath the stars, beside the fire, next to his shelter.

As he slept, many creatures from the forest came to gaze upon him: The grizzly bear and mountain lion, the raccoon and elk, predator and prey. His gentle and loving spirit drew them, calling to their yearning hearts.

One night, a few days later, Hakan came to Aiyana's shelter. She bade him enter and listened to his entreaty.

"You are of age, Aiyana, and it is time to choose a man to marry and start a family. I am a good man, I will provide for you, protect you, surround you with love forever," he said.

Aiyana looked at her feet, then back to Hakan. "My answer is the same as when you asked before. We are friends, but I will never marry you. Be at peace with my answer and find another to start your family."

"But you are alone. You have no family, your father now one year gone. Let me protect you. Other maidens long for my attention. Why are you indifferent?"

Aiyana's eyes flashed at the mention of her father. "My father was a great fighter. He battled the North Wind, he fought the Gitchigumi itself, and his spirit lives in me. I don't need your protection or anyone's."

Hakan shook his head in frustration that she would reject him, and silently decided that someone else had stolen her heart. Bitter jealousy and rage took root inside him.

"But, why?" he asked, palms open and extended.

She shook her head and looked away. "You have my answer once again, and for the last time. Please go now."

Scowling, Hakan left to fan the embers smoldering inside him.

In the yellow light of a candle, Aiyana stood motionless. She thought of the Stranger, a warrior who spoke with restrained, controlled power, whose body and mind seemed balanced like the world's own center, but whose movements were like mist skimming a pond's glassy surface. She had watched him carefully when he had appeared in the village. Every movement, every glance, every word he spoke, every choice to remain silent when others would have spoken, had entranced her.

She wanted to be a warrior like him. She wanted his grace and supple strength. She longed to fight for something more than herself and something greater than her village, as great as the wide and deep sky.

She sat on a stool before a mirror. Taking a sharp knife, she cut her hair close to her scalp.

The next day, the Stranger sat cross-legged on the shore of the great lake and whittled the tip of a tree limb into a spear. On his shoulder perched a falcon. The falcon turned to look and gave a call. Some hundred yards distant, Aiyana approached. She wore the simple clothing of a warrior: a tunic and trousers made of caribou hide, with a knife upon her hip.

The falcon flew off, and the Stranger stood as Aiyana stopped before him. She nodded to him and he nodded in return. She knelt on the beach before the crashing waves. The Stranger sat, accepting her presence, and returned to his whittling, while Aiyana rested her hands in her lap.

"A true warrior always fights to protect. What do you wish to protect?" he asked, as his gleaming knife cast shavings to the sand.

"Everything."

He laughed. "Would you protect the newborn hare from the wolf?"

"Yes!"

"But the wolf must eat to live."

Aiyana paused, choosing her words carefully. "I want to protect the helpless from the powerful."

The Stranger glanced at her. "That's better. Always remember this: the wolf and the falcon kill, but they are not evil. The evil in this world is brought here by human beings. Now go home and return in the morning."

Aiyana stared. She reached to touch his cheek, for she felt great affection and gratitude toward him, but he grasped her wrist to stop her.

"Our kinship is of the spirit. I will teach you what I know because we are from the same family of warriors. We can be friends, because the meaning of friendship is sharing beautiful and true things with one another. But that is all we can be." He released her wrist and returned his attention to his spear.

Aiyana nodded and left.

The next morning, she returned as he had asked. Day after day, week after week, she came to him and he taught her all he knew of the world and of being a warrior. Sometimes she spent the night asleep in his shelter while he slept under the moon and stars beside it. Over time, the creatures around the Stranger came to know and trust her. Gradually, the warm summer days turned to cool autumn.

Every day, Hakan followed her from a distance. He watched the two of them from a far dune hidden behind bushes. His rage and jealousy grew and grew, seemingly boundless. He spread lies and rumors about Aiyana and the Stranger among the villagers, for the rage twisted his heart, deforming it.

One day, warriors from a distant village approached along the coast having heard that the grown men of the village were gone, and the people were easy prey.

The Stranger and Aiyana, with the help of the wolves, the grizzly bear, the falcon, and the mountain lion fought a great battle and drove them away. Aiyana fought with fire in her chest, righteous and calm, knowing she was protecting the weak from the powerful, for it was what she was born to do.

Hakan watched the battle from afar, hidden and trembling. He could not be happy for the victory. He watched Aiyana leave the Stranger behind and return to the village alone to deliver the news. He followed her and approached her before she reached the village.

Hakan had a false smile on his face and opened his arms as if to embrace her. She returned his smile, unaware of the hatred in him, and stepped forward. But Hakan took his knife and thrust it into her trusting heart.

Aiyana's eyes grew wide like a full moon. Her spirit left her body for the sky. As her empty body slumped toward the ground, Hakan held it up in his arms, tears in his eyes. He released her and ran toward the village. Above, the falcon screamed, gyred, and flew to the Stranger.

Once in the village, Hakan called loudly. The villagers ran from their dwellings and surrounded him. He told them that he had seen the Stranger kill Aiyana, and they wailed in grief.

Back by the lake, the Stranger followed the falcon and came to Aiyana's body, lying beside Gitchigumi. He suspected at once what had happened. He clenched his fists and ground his teeth. His face burned scarlet.

But then the anger drained from his body into the vast lake which took his pain and fury away and returned calmness, love, and peace. The Stranger bent and placed his hands beneath her shoulders and legs, lifted her, and carried her body toward the village.

The crowd of villagers glared at him as he approached. Hakan stood to the side, pointed at the Stranger, and shouted, "Murderer!"

The Stranger stopped before them and laid Aiyana's body on the ground. The silent villagers stared, fearful now of him.

The Village Elder stepped forward. "Hakan says you have killed Aiyana. What do you have to say for yourself, Stranger?"

"Don't let him speak! He doesn't deserve to speak. He deserves punishment!" cried Hakan.

"Silence!" snapped the Elder. To the Stranger she said quietly, "Speak now."

The Stranger opened his hands and arms and bowed to the villagers.

"This child fought a great battle to protect you. She is a daughter of this entire village, and she fought bravely with love in her heart. She was a true warrior whom you must never forget, as you have forgotten me." He dropped to one knee before Aiyana's body and bowed his head.

"I never touched this child except with chaste affection, nor have I taken her life. Believe whom you must, and I will yield to whatever judgement you levy against me. But give this great warrior, whose body lies before you, the funeral and burial of a hero."

"He is a liar! I saw with my own eyes how he killed her!" screamed Hakan. The Stranger did not reply, but remained quiet and motionless, his head bowed.

The villagers stared at the Stranger. They looked to Hakan, who shook and struck his thighs with his fists.

After a moment's silence, the Village Elder reached out and placed her palm gently on the Stranger's head.

"I remember now. Many years ago, as you carried Aiyana, you carried our mother's body into our village. We sent you to find the killers and grant justice. I am your sister. Welcome home, my brother," she said.

Another old woman stepped forward. "Welcome home, brother."

A young woman also stepped forward. "I am your daughter, we are all your daughters, your sisters, and your family. Welcome home."

All the villagers gathered around at last and echoed, "Welcome home."

"You are fools!" shouted Hakan. "I don't need this village. I don't need *any* of you. You are all strangers to me," he declared with contempt. He turned and began to stroll away from the village.

The Village Elder bent low and whispered to the Stranger, "Grant us justice, one more time, for Aiyana."

The Stranger whistled. Four giant falcons flew from the four corners of the world. Their wings thundered upon the air. They fell on Hakan and tore him to pieces.

The villagers gathered the man who was no longer a stranger into their arms and kissed his cheek.

"Tell us your name now, that we may know you again," said the Village Elder.

"My name is Nanabosho. My journey is over at last."

Chapter Seventeen

You can't force the world to rhyme

~Elizabeth

They sat in silence for a long time. Finally, Elizabeth asked "Is the story true?"

"Do you want it to be?"

She nearly said no. But she realized that the story made her feel strong and warm.

"Yes," she whispered.

"Then of course it is true," answered Jamu.

Closing her eyes, Elizabeth imagined Aiyana's warrior courage, the great battle, the powerful and vast lake, Gitchigumi. She thought of how horrible jealousy can be and how it can twist people's hearts. She thought about how important family can be.

"Who told you this story?"

"Follow me. I have something for you to see."

Elizabeth followed Jamu, who scurried to a small opening in the cave wall and disappeared inside. She emerged dragging something behind her. It was a circular object decorated with beads and feathers with a weave in the middle, attached to a leather necklace.

Elizabeth examined the exquisite and fragile item. "What is it?"

"A dreamcatcher, worn by a dream weaver. Someone left it for you years ago, when passing this way. He told me you would come one day."

"For me? Who left it?"

"Your father, my dear."

"My father was here?"

Jamu nodded. "Yes, he was here in a frantic state. He was searching for you, but for you it was too early, and for him, too late." Elizabeth looked more closely at the dreamcatcher. Something about it was familiar. Something about her father, about keeping out bad dreams. Her hands shook.

"What is a dream weaver?" She placed the dreamcatcher around her neck.

"A dream weaver is someone who sleeps so deeply that they cannot wake. A dream weaver creates a world from dreams as real and true as anything in the world of those awake. Your father wore this dreamcatcher too and told me of Nanabosho, which I have now told to you."

"How did he know I would be here?"

"In dreams," said Jamu, "*now* is when it should be. All the seconds come all at once, not just one, two, or three."

Elizabeth nodded. "And in the world of those awake,

seconds come one after the other, and time's long, like a snake."

Jamu nodded. "You learn quickly, and your mind wanders free. Your father saw the snake as it bit its tail. In dreams he succeeded, while awake he would fail."

"He died, didn't he? And Gichi Manidoo proves that death is a kind of dream, right?"

"The truth will come in its own time. You can't force the world to rhyme."

Jamu scurried up the side of Elizabeth's body, and stopped on her head. Elizabeth looked up. Jamu made upside-down eye contact with her.

"I will always be with you in my heart, as your father is, little warrior peanut-thief," said Jamu. "Now let me teach you to waltz and help you shed your grief."

Jamu scampered off and stood on her hind legs beside her.

Elizabeth shook her head. "I don't think I want to dance, Jamu. I want to know how my father came to be here. I want to know where *here* is. I want to know where my mother is. I want to know who I am. And where is Zaagi? I'm sorry, but I want out of this cave, Jamu. The world is dying, you know. We have to climb the mountain. Jiibay said so."

"No climbing in a storm like this. Learn to dance before you climb, or the steps of life you'll miss." Jamu weaved from side to side. Her body leaned as her head tipped first one way, and then the other. "When we use rhythm and melody to move through space, then body and spirit will unite with grace."

She watched Jamu's sinuous movement, mesmerized. "Okay. You can teach me. But I won't be patient forever."

Jamu nodded and showed her the steps of a waltz, and Elizabeth copied her. She drew her right foot back, then pulled both feet together, forming a box. After repeating the steps for several minutes, Jamu scampered up and sat on her left shoulder.

"Pretend you have a handsome boy in your arms, enchanted by your wit and charms," she whispered. Elizabeth pretended to take a hand in her right hand and to rest her left arm over an imagined sturdy shoulder. "Now, as I've taught you, take a chance, and with this gentle partner, let's learn to dance."

Jamu hummed the tune of a waltz. Elizabeth took a deep breath and held it, cleared her mind, and took the first step. She stumbled, righted herself, and kept going. She breathed again. After a bit, the movement became natural.

Jamu whispered, "What's your partner's name? A story without details is a shame."

"His name is—Fede," she decided. She closed her eyes and imagined him completely. "His eyes are blue and deep, his skin is brown like the bark of an oak tree. His hair is curly and soft.

He wears glasses that are too large and his nose is long and curved. He broke it in a fall when he was trying to ride a wild horse."

Jamu interrupted her humming to laugh. "So brave, your lad. But foolish, perhaps, and hasty just a tad?"

"Just a tad," admitted Elizabeth. "He's clumsy and shy. He claims he writes poetry. I think he's going to pass out from holding his breath, he's so nervous."

"Poor Fede. Now stop and let him bow. You curtsy in return. Enough for now."

Elizabeth complied as Jamu left her shoulder and returned to the top of her large boulder.

Elizabeth came close. "Thank you, Jamu." Then she saw Jamu's glistening eyes. "Oh. Are you alright?"

"I've never left this cave, or danced with anyone, long or brief. Since my birth so long ago, this cave is a prison, as fate provided so. But always remember this—stories are bridges, they take us where we need to go, but they aren't our journey's end, you know." Then Jamu turned and disappeared once more behind the boulder.

Elizabeth sighed and returned to rest on her ferns.

She was sleepy, and her shoulder began to ache. She rubbed it, laid back, and curled into a ball. The sound of rain was a thousand footsteps of a sad and lonely walk home in her heart.

Chapter Eighteen

I don't need your boat

~Federico

I leaned against a wall with my arms folded and watched people – mostly hospital staff – enter and exit from the Intensive Care Unit. The to-and-fro motion of the two automated swinging doors was almost hypnotic. I tightened my grip on the manila envelope I held in my left hand, reminding myself of my purpose here. A woman in her early thirties with short, gray hair and a reddened, splotchy face exited as she wiped her eyes with a balled-up tissue. A group of three doctors in white coats with stethoscopes hanging around their necks laughed at some joke amongst themselves as they swept past the woman and through the swinging doors.

I walked to a small waiting area with upholstered chairs surrounded by plastic ferns. I sat in a chair where I could watch the ICU door. Crossing my legs, I set the envelope on a little table and picked up a magazine instead. I thumbed through it, pretending to look at the perfect people in perfect houses doing beautiful things together.

I'd walked through the swinging doors a half hour ago and had been immediately stopped by a friendly but stern nurse who couldn't possibly have been out of her teens. A tattooed tear-drop clung to the corner of her eye. She'd asked me where I was headed. I told her Marie Mulligan's room. She frowned and told me visiting hours were over and, besides, visitors had been restricted to her husband only. I apologized and turned to go. She'd asked my name as I walked away and I'd pretended not to hear her.

After a few minutes of watching the door, a woman with black hair in a tight bun, and who wore a brown uniform, caught my eye. She kept her eyes cast down demurely, a look I recognized as belonging to the servant class, hired domestic workers with few options, and the class to which I belonged. Each time she entered, she pushed a cart loaded with various clean linens and each time she exited, the cart was full of soiled towels and sheets.

When I saw her more closely, my palms began to sweat. Heat rushed up my neck. *Sister Guadalupe Hidalgo.* I knew it couldn't possibly be the scourge of *Santa Maria de la Paz* middle school, but my eyes told me otherwise.

I recalled the hooded eyes framed by crows-feet, the purple spots covering her clawed hands. She had a knack of materializing, invariably, like a silent predator behind me in her black habit whenever I was involved in or contemplating even the smallest mischief. Most of all, I remembered the stinging smacks of the ruler on my upturned, open palms. I could almost see the deep frown lines and hear the swift swish as she delivered blow after blow. Tears began to burn at the corners of my eyes from just the memory. *Dios te salve, María, llena eres de gracia...*

I'm not sure what possessed me, but I stood and walked up to her as she waited with a load of clean linens for the ICU door to open. She glanced at me, then hesitated. I smiled. Up close, the resemblance to Sister Guadalupe retreated. She was younger than her, and her eyes were softer and kinder, whereas the Sister's eyes were hard and focused with stringent clarity. I took a deep breath.

"Can I help you?" she asked. A nametag headed "Housekeeping," gave her name as "Isabel." I tried to speak, but the words caught in my throat. I wasn't sure what I wanted to say. I knew I needed to talk to her, that it was important. Now that I stood before her, though, words escaped me.

She squinted at me as I stared at her face. She wore no makeup. There were wrinkles on her forehead, around her eyes, and at the corners of her mouth. It seemed to me they were the kind of dignified wrinkles purchased by a hard life, and she appeared to wear them unashamedly and openly. *If only* she *had been my Sister Guadalupe...*

She coughed and touched my arm, motioning for me to step with her to the side. She pushed her cart against the wall, and we walked to a small alcove that held an ATM machine.

"You're Federico, aren't you," she said with a smile that quickly disappeared. She held her small hand out. "I'm Isabel, Marie's friend. We work... used to work together." Her voice was resonant and full. I hesitated only for a second and shook her hand.

"She told you about me? How is she? I'd like to see her."

"Yes, she told me about you before the... accident. But it may not be good for you to see her, Federico. If her husband found out..." She looked at the floor.

I touched her shoulder and furrowed my brow. "I don't care about her husband. I need to see her. Help me. *Por favor?*"

She looked up. The look in her eyes sent a jolt through me as I sensed something slipping away, just like it had once before.

My mind wrenched me from the present into the past, into that other moment. I was beside a little brook that ran through a section of a cemetery. My mother was being buried as an indigent among other pauper graves. I was eight. I kept thinking the lid on the cheap pine box would pop open, she'd step out, and tell me she was sorry for playing a trick on me. The Padre had handed me a little paper boat, perhaps thinking it would keep me from crying. As he said "*Que descanse en paz,*" he made the sign of the cross over the box. That was when I knew it meant goodbye. I dropped to my knees and tossed the boat into the nearby brook. I put both my hands into the icy water and dug them into the mud. *I don't need your boat, Mama doesn't need your boat.* It floated away as the Social Worker took my hand and pulled me up from the stream. I pulled and twisted my arm, trying to escape, and wiped mud with my free hand on her yellow dress. But she dragged me away from the grave as I kicked and screamed.

"Marie is giving up," Isabel said, dragging me back into the present. "*Lo siento.*"

"No."

Isabel raised an eyebrow. "Listen to me. Remember her the way she was when you last saw her." She put her hand on my shoulder and leaned in close. "Her body is shutting down. There is no way to reach her. To see her connected to those machines… no," she shook her head, "it's better you go home now, Federico."

A doctor stepped up to the ATM machine behind us. She had long blonde hair and horn-rimmed glasses. She glanced at us. We fell silent, waiting for her to finish her transaction and leave.

I held up the manila envelope and offered it to Isabel. "Please."

She hesitated but took it from me.

"She told me you were a writer. You want me to give her your story, *si?*"

"It's *her* story."

"Ah. Very well. I promise you that I will make sure she gets it, if you will promise me to go home now." I nodded my thanks and she stepped close to hug me. The hug was warm and full. She smelled of hand sanitizer and the musky cinnamon odor of *arroz con leche*. I smiled at her and turned to leave.

"I will pray to Saint Jude for Marie," she called to me from behind. The patron saint of desperate and lost causes.

Outside the hospital, a chilly autumn rain came down hard. In the parking lot, I watched a small river of rainwater rush over my feet. As I reached my car, I clenched my fists and fought the urge to smash my foot into the fender. The rain changed to hail. It stung and cooled my skin. My face to the sky, the rage retreated again to the deep place inside where it lived.

Remember her the way she was...

Chapter Nineteen

Just a kiss, one kiss, and I'll be gone

~Elizabeth

Day and night, the rain continued without stopping. Two days passed and still Zaagi had not returned for her. She decided that in one more day, if Zaagi didn't return, she would leave the cave to find him even if it meant braving the terrible storm that still crashed outside. Her concern for her furry friend was causing her to lose sleep, but Jamu was a welcome distraction.

After playfully chasing Jamu around the cave, Elizabeth laid on her stomach, winded. Jamu lay down, facing her. She was worried that she nearly caught Jamu, for today Jamu seemed lethargic and not herself.

Elizabeth interlaced her fingers and leaned in until she was almost nose-to-nose with Jamu. Thunder resounded from the far distance. *Maybe I'm near the center of things that the coyote told me about,* she thought. *Maybe the center isn't a place in the world, but a place in the heart.* Her own heart pounded.

"How old are you, Jamu?" she asked. Each breath she exhaled ruffled Jamu's fur and made it shimmer in the blue light.

"As old as the wind, as old as the honey bee, as old as the

newborn child, as old as an ancient and failing sequoia tree."

"That is old and young. Why do you always rhyme when you speak?"

"To rhyme is sublime. It's a dance with words, a murmuration of birds, it reminds us that play is the meaning of life, not discord or strife. Will you rhyme for me? Will you let your words waltz and tango? Make them sound so sweet, like the papaya and the mango."

"Not this time. Maybe later I'll learn to rhyme," Elizabeth said and winked. Jamu giggled.

The chipmunk walked up the incline toward the opening to the cave. Elizabeth followed. Jamu's movements were usually quick and nimble. Today, each step of her tiny paws came after a hesitation, as if she couldn't find the strength to go forward.

Jamu sat at the lip of the cave and watched the rain. Elizabeth sat beside her. A bolt of lightning struck nearby with a bang so loud that Elizabeth jumped. Her hair stood up on her arms as if her brain was warning her of something unpleasant.

Jamu walked from the edge of the cave's overhang into the rain. Her fur was so wet it looked like gloss as she turned and held Elizabeth's gaze while Jamu's ears hung, heavy and sodden.

"I'm sorry, Elizabeth. It's time for me to go. I'm full, and the circle is complete. But in your heart, you know that only you can set me free. I want to sleep and dream the world. I want to leave this cave, this cage, this everlasting grave. The moon calls to me, the streams whisper, and the stars are singing to me. Release me so I can go to them."

Elizabeth's stomach twisted like a wet rope. Standing, she clenched her hands into fists. "I'm still a child. How can you ask me to do this?"

"You must, Elizabeth," Jamu said. "I've waited for you forever. You are my *Marwolaeth*. Now you are here, and I need you. It's nothing, really. Just a kiss, one kiss and I'll be gone. It's what love is, it's the heart of Gichi Manidoo, and it's the circle at the center of the forever dance."

Elizabeth pointed to the glowing diamonds in the ceiling of the cave. "But who will tell the stories if you're gone? I can't do it, Jamu. I'm a failure at remembering. And why have you stopped rhyming?" She searched for any argument she could muster. "You've never left this cave. Aren't you terrified?"

Jamu nodded. Water droplets clung to her chin, elongated, and fell like glass flower petals. She smiled. "A little. You are rare and blessed and will have the chance to see and touch and know the whole world, not just hear about it in stories. You don't have to remember my stories, you can tell your own. Now I will tell you Zaagi's words. But first, you must make the storm stop."

Elizabeth frowned. "How will I make it stop?"

"By knowing it is time for it to stop."

Elizabeth looked to the rain-drenched sky. She shivered, wrapped her arms around herself, and rocked from side to side. She nodded, and inside she knew Jamu was right. She cleared her mind, focused on the warmth and brightness of the sapphire sky she first saw when walking out of the darkness. She remembered the whisper of the minnows in the stream, and the song flowed through her body and into the air around her.

The rain stopped.

The clouds dissolved and the sun burst through, brilliant and blinding. She shielded her eyes. It warmed her skin. Her tight shoulders relaxed, and her breathing slowed. She stepped outside the cave, sat in front of Jamu, and crossed her legs.

"Please tell me," Elizabeth said.

Jamu stood. She used her paw to smooth her ears, like Zaagi did. She hopped on her hind legs a few times, mimicking his impatient habit.

"I am fine, silly girl. You are not lost because you are right where you are, and needn't worry!" Jamu said, imitating Zaagi's voice. "I am straightening out broken stems and mending the weave in my heart, and I will come back to you when the sun returns and bring you something sweet."

Elizabeth forgot for a moment that it was Jamu speaking, so perfectly did Jamu imitate his speech and habits. "What should I do, Zaagi? You're wise and grown up."

"Do what you know you must do. If there is no one to listen, why would the moon speak, or the streams whisper, or the stars sing? Free Jamu who longs to listen to them, and we will free Bellflower, find your family and kill the black snake that eats the world."

Jamu looked into Elizabeth's eyes.

Elizabeth looked up at the sky, so blue and deep. It was the same sky she remembered seeing when she first found Zaagi. She didn't want to look into Jamu's eyes and lose her, not just yet.

She closed her eyes and saw her mother's face in her memory-painting, asleep, inches from her. The yellow curtain over her mother's shoulder billowed, and a warm breeze enveloped them.

Her mother stirred and opened her eyes. She gazed at Elizabeth, her eyes still dreamy. She reached out, caressed her forehead, and kissed her.

"I love you," her mother whispered.

"I love you, too," Elizabeth whispered back. She opened her eyes, leaned forward, and kissed Jamu on her forehead.

"Goodbye, Jamu."

"Thank you, thank you. Now one last thing," said Jamu. "Your name's not *Elizabeth*, you see. Your chosen name is *Marie*; Elizabeth Marie, your name upon your birth. Remember it, now born again in Gichi Manidoo, with memories new upon this earth. Goodbye, Marie, my injured and dreaming peanut-thief. And remember, sometimes cages can protect us until we're ready to be free."

Chapter Twenty

Diary - 9/23/2006

~Marie

I've just come up to Mount Pleasant from MSU in Lansing, from the nursing program that has taken up most of my life. I've been visiting my mother.

I'm writing in my parked car with the windows rolled up because it's raining so hard. The damned air conditioning isn't working right, and my thighs and back are drenched.

I can see her room from where I'm parked. I can see the very window itself. It's a modern building, well-appointed, clean, crisp, and cold. Casino revenues do wonderful things. She has a private room to herself, where she lies in a metal-framed bed propped on embroidered pillows. A TV directly in front of her has "The Price is Right" blaring.

"Come on down!"

I said, "Mom, I met a man. He's going to take care of me. He said he'll protect me forever and keep me safe. His name's Carl. I know he loves me. I just have to teach him a few things, Mom. Teach him to give me just a little more freedom. A little more trust. His grip's too tight, too confining sometimes. But he's what I need right now, you know? I think I love him.

That's the truth, and the truth is what I say it is. You know me. Goodbye, Mom. You told me it only takes two to make a family. I have a new one, so don't worry about me."

I gave her the pills she asked for months ago.

She didn't reach for them when I held them out. I took her hand in mine, spilled the pills into her palm, and closed her fingers. She mouthed something, and sound came out—a hoarse whisper. I wasn't sure what she was trying to tell me. It didn't really matter.

The pills will kill her. Perhaps they already have. I've been sitting here in this sweltering damn car, waiting, for a long time.

As I stood over her, I noticed her arm was twisted to the side, pushed up by something beneath it. I carefully raised her arm and pulled out a frayed stuffed animal. It had been mine when I was younger. A movie called *The Lion King* had come out and one of the characters was my favorite. It was a talking meerkat called Timon. The black-circled eyes stared back at me accusingly. Small tufts of cotton poked through a frayed seam in its side. I laid it across her chest as if it were napping. She stirred and opened her eyes.

I kissed her cool forehead, in a hurry to leave, so I could sit in this exhaust-belching metal coffin and wait. Her eyes were grateful, but distant, already somewhere no one else can follow. I couldn't meet anyone else's eyes when I walked down the corridor to the elevator. Is this how we leave cages, always with death?

Soon, they'll find her and call me. I think I need to throw up, but I can't. Mom, I hurt so much. It's in my chest, it's in my heart. I promise you I'll never hurt anyone else like this, I'll never leave them alone, I'll never abandon them.

On the seat beside me is Grandma Aki's dreamcatcher.

Mom handed it to me as I was leaving. It's supposed to catch bad dreams that prowl through the world from slipping into our heads and keep us safe as we sleep. I remember falling asleep as a little girl with it hanging over me. And just before I'd fall asleep, I'd try to send my dreams through it the other way, the other direction out into the world, like a note in a bottle, to find another girl or boy who needed loving dreams in their lives.

There it is. My phone is ringing.

I don't belong anywhere anymore.

Chapter Twenty-One

Everything we love below depends on how we fall

~*Elizabeth*

Elizabeth stood before the cave and then walked some distance away before turning to look back at the entrance. It was set in a giant slab of rust-colored granite that rose high above her. The granite slab was part of the base of a towering mountain, Mount Beldurra she assumed. Next to the cave opening, rough-hewn steps led upward and zig-zagged across the face of the mountain. They disappeared behind a rock overhang thousands of feet above. The path forked at the cave's entrance.

She shrugged and took the path to the left that followed the base of the mountain. After about five minutes of walking, she came to a cave opening. A willow tree grew nearby with a patch of strawberries beneath it. She frowned. The mountain was gigantic. She couldn't possibly have circled it.

She sighed and took the path to the right. Five minutes later, the cave opening, and willow tree appeared again. She continued. The same cave entrance appeared again.

How could she be moving in circles if the path never

curved, she wondered. She folded her arms. The only way to get past the mountain, it appeared, was over it. She furrowed her brow and pursed her lips.

She turned and looked behind her. The path she was on split the center of a field of knee-high grass which was dotted with yellow and lavender flowers. In the far distance, a stand of oak trees stood guard over the field. It was totally quiet. A breeze swelled and smoothed back her hair and brushed the tips of the grass in delicate waves. The sweet scent of violets wafted over her.

She tilted her head and heard a high-pitched hiss in the distance. She stood still and listened as its volume increased to a screechy buzz.

A tiny head poked up from the grass at intervals. As the creature neared, the buzzing got louder, too. When she saw the face, her skin warmed and her shoulders relaxed.

She folded her arms and frowned as Zaagi bounded toward her. He shouted and gesticulated but was still too far away for her to understand him. A cup? The sun? His wife? A sun for his wife in a cup? A brown cloud swirled and buzzed close behind him.

As Zaagi approached, the buzzing intensified. She squinted. She recognized the cloud boiling behind him, a giant swarm of angry bees. About fifty yards away, his cries became clear at last.

"Run! Run, Elizabeth! Run for your life! Up the mountain. Up, up!"

Her heart raced as she rushed to the base of the mountain and started up the wide, hewn steps of the stairway. She glanced over her shoulder. Zaagi reached the base, and the bees began to close in. She climbed until her calves burned and sweat dripped into her eyes from her forehead.

She stopped on an outcropping of granite that jutted five or six feet away from the cliff wall. She dropped to her hands and knees and peered over the edge. Zaagi clambered up toward her as a small cloud of bees buzzed around his head. She lay prone, reached her hand down, and waited. Zaagi hopped high and planted his paw in her hand. She grasped it hard and hauled him onto the ledge with her. The remaining bees hovered, hummed, and retreated down the side of the mountain.

She reached her hand out to grasp a handhold on the ledge above her and yanked it back. There was a yawning black hole where the rock's lip had been. She had nearly put her hand into it. Debris fell on her head as the hole grew larger.

She skirted to the side of the steps and pulled herself up and past the churning black maw. Zaagi followed easily, his breath wheezing from his snout.

Meerkat and girl climbed into the sky. The steps grew steeper and narrower. More black holes appeared and turned their frantic ascent into a gauntlet. Both kept the cool granite wall within touch, eyes always forward and upward. After twenty minutes or so, her breath labored and chest heaving, she heard a plaintive call behind her.

"Elizabeth! Elizabeth?"

"Not now, Zaagi. We need to get to the top first, my friend."

A ledge appeared ahead, an outcropping of thick rock that interrupted the steps. The ledge hung out at least eight feet over the abyss. She crested the top step, staggered against the wall of the mountain, and bent over. She braced, hands on knees. Her drenched t-shirt clung to her torso and sweat rolled off the bridge of her nose. She glanced down the side of the mountain. Rock and tumbling boulders slid down in a roar of debris as the mountain was chewed by thousands of the churning black disks.

She panted for a few moments before she straightened herself and looked at Zaagi. She shook her head and sighed. Zaagi crawled toward her, his ears against his head, tears streaming down his face.

Reaching out, she took him into her arms and rocked him. He snuggled into her shoulder and closed his eyes. He was warm and he shivered, relaxed, and then shivered again.

She noticed his fur was splotched with gobs of honey; the "sweet" thing he had promised he'd bring to her. She scooped a small dollop from his forehead with a finger and tasted it. It was spicy, thick, and gently sweet.

"Marwolaeth?" she asked. Zaagi opened his eyes and gazed out at the horizon.

"I bid him adieu," he said quietly, and then snuggled closer. Her breathing slowed.

Ahead, the mountain's shadow cast itself over a distant

forest as evening came upon them and the sun set somewhere behind. Above, misty clouds drifted close. Elizabeth imagined she could reach out and scoop out a handful of fluff. She stroked Zaagi's fur.

She knew they were at the peak.

The giant mountain shivered and tilted briefly, then settled back. Dusk retreated into night as the stars shone in the sky like windows inviting them into the heavens. Each one blazed with a gentle warmth, each one was eager to tell a loving secret or break a heart.

Sing to me, Elizabeth thought to the stars. *I deserve to hear you, don't I? I have nothing left, for I've lost my memory, my family. I have nothing except this beautiful, sad meerkat with a broken heart, a meerkat who's in love with a dream. Is she real? Does she love him too? Please let it be so. I don't know if I have the strength left to save us both.*

One star shone brighter and began to grow. It expanded until it was as large as a full moon. The star stopped and hovered over her. She gently put Zaagi on the ground without waking him and stood. The star stretched and contracted until it rearranged itself into the image of Jiibay's smiling face. His eyes were pure white and glimmered.

"Sister," he said.

"Brother," Elizabeth said, since the word "sister" brought her memory of Parker back in a flood—Parker's prized fishing pole that she and her parents had picked out for his birthday, the two young mourning doves they had both nursed to health after the doves fell from their nest, the way he always seemed to know what she was going to say, as if he could see into the future.

"Nobody will save you, except yourself. Those who dream and those who are dreamed become one, and yet go their own way. Tell your story there to Federico, so that Marie will hear and remember."

She nodded and stepped closer to Jiibay and the cliff edge.

"You mean *my* Federico? The boy I danced with?"

"Here, let me show you," Jiibay said. He retreated from the cliff. She closed her eyes and followed, stepping into the void. She floated into a tunnel of sapphires. She saw through Marie's vantage point as she walked downstairs into a familiar boiler room. She saw Federico sneeze and wipe his nose on his sleeve, and look up at her, embarrassed.

"Can I help you?" he asked with a gentle but deep voice. A large, husky man with powerful shoulders, he was dressed in blue denim and an open cowboy shirt. A receding hairline atop a large forehead gave him an air of wisdom, and his blue eyes sparkled with wit and humor. He had been Elizabeth's dance partner as a young boy in the cave.

"Can *I* help *you?*" Marie asked.

"I'm sorry, miss, but you're trespassing."

"No, I'm not. I own this house," she said.

"I know Carl Mulligan owns this property," he said. "And you are his… daughter?" Marie raised an eyebrow. "Sister?"

"I'm his wife, Marie."

"I'm sorry to hear that," he said. He shook his head and blushed.

Marie smiled. "Thank you. And you are…?"

"Federico. Federico Garcia. I'm the realtor your husband hired."

Music played from the phone in Federico's pocket; a Spanish waltz. Marie began to sway.

He took a step closer. "You're a dancer?" he asked.

"Someone taught me how to waltz once," she said, and also stepped closer. She was eager to dance with him once again, with the memory of Jamu perched on her shoulder.

His eyes widened, and he said, "I know how to waltz." She pulled him closer, placing her hands in position, and began to move. As they danced to the hushed percussion of steam, she noticed he held his breath. He stepped clumsily on her left foot and his face reddened.

"It doesn't matter," Marie said. "It doesn't hurt."

After their dance, Elizabeth withdrew from Marie, and Jiibay brought her back through the tunnel of sapphires to the mountain peak.

She sat beside Zaagi, who stirred, stretched, and curled up against her thigh. "That was Fede, grown up," she said. "I think he's falling in love with me—I mean with Marie."

Jiibay smiled. "Yes, but she's a married woman. Now it's time for you to step from the edge with your friend to find his Bellflower. But the choice to be found and freed will be Bellflower's, not Zaagi's and not yours. You cannot save someone who is not ready to be saved."

"Will you come to me again?"

"This is goodbye, for either Marie will break the bond and I will be free, or we will all perish with her as this world ends. You are all Marie has left. You must hurry, for even now it may be too late."

A deep rumble pulsed through her body. She turned her head to look behind her and began to tremble. The black disk in the sky was gigantic—it ate nearly a quarter of the stars in the heavens and was growing.

Jiibay faded into his star and the star receded to take its place in the chorus of light.

She stood and turned to see Zaagi standing beside her. He reached his paw up. She stooped slightly and grasped it in her hand. They looked around. They were at the peak. There were only two choices. On one side of the mountain was a void that led to the outside. On the other side, the steps led back down to the churning black holes that ate everything in their path. A tearing, wrenching crack exploded under their feet as the mountain began to disintegrate.

"Which way, Elizabeth?" Zaagi asked.

"Forward." she answered. Zaagi nodded. Together, they stepped out into the empty air.

Chapter Twenty-Two

The Joshua Tree

~Elizabeth

A crescent moon hung like a fiddle's bow. It glowed against

the night's otherwise absolute blackness and illuminated the desert landscape where plum-colored mountains hunkered at the horizon. The sky was starless.

Elizabeth sat in the warm sand and looked into the eyes of Marie. Elizabeth was dressed in her red t-shirt and jeans and wore her dreamcatcher around her neck. Marie wore a white cotton hospital gown, speckled with tiny pink roses. Matted hair clung to the older woman's swollen, pasty face. Her eyes were hooded and cloudy. A thick bandage curled around from just above her ear to the back of her head. Elizabeth barely recognized herself in this grown woman who sat across from her.

They sat with their legs folded beneath them, facing each other. They extended their arms and wrapped their hands around one another's wrists. Their arms formed a circle. On the ground between them flickered a small, pale flame.

Something in Elizabeth's mind shifted, like a mirror reflecting another mirror's image. She saw herself through Marie's eyes—a young girl with short hair and wide eyes. The mirror shifted again, and once more she was inside herself.

"Where are we?" Elizabeth asked. "When are we?"

"In between, I think," Marie said. Each word sounded heavy.

Elizabeth looked past Marie's shoulder. A single tree rose about six feet from the ground and then sprouted a tangle of limbs that curled around each other, reaching for the sky. Each limb ended with a hand or glove of thin green leaves pointed to the sky. She looked at Marie, who was staring at the tree as well.

"It looks like it's praying," Marie said, looking back at Elizabeth.

"You remember," Elizabeth said.

"It's a Joshua tree."

Elizabeth smiled. "Mom and Dad took us camping here with Parker." Their grip loosened and relaxed then tightened again. They rocked in unison, forward and back.

"Help me. Help us," Elizabeth whispered. Her shoulders shook. "If you let me go, you can save us both."

Marie looked down at the flame, which had gotten smaller, weaker, almost like a match flame. She closed her eyes and her chin fell on her chest. The silent air seemed heavy and thick.

Elizabeth jerked her hands hard, almost pulling Marie into the tiny flame. Marie's eyes flashed open and the flame grew.

"Wake up, Marie! Wake up now!"

"I'll lose you forever," Marie said, averting her eyes. Elizabeth could feel the fear, the sheer terror of losing everything coming through Marie's hands. She'd felt it herself.

"I'll find you. I know how to cross over now. I'll tell Federico the story."

"No. You can never be in the same place with me;

everything will fall apart. It's a dance, Elizabeth. I'm dancing and I'm at my limit now, I can't sustain both of us in one place. And I'm very, very tired."

Marie's body slumped forward, her head dropped over the small flame and soft saffron light danced on her face. Elizabeth lowered her head and leaned forward until their foreheads touched, the flame licking at their chins.

"Fede," Elizabeth said simply.

Marie's eyes jerked open and they flashed like sparks. She shook her head.

"I think he's broken inside, Elizabeth."

"I think so, too." Elizabeth nodded. "He thinks he can't let anyone see him like that. He hides it even from himself."

"He will help me—will help us," Elizabeth said, pulling her head up, excitement rising in her voice. "Fede can help keep *him* away from you, can tell you our story after I've told it to him, and you will heal yourself, will…"

Marie raised her head and shook it. "Fede has his own problems. Involving him would be using him."

"He's in love with you. He's trying to save himself with stories, too."

Marie refocused her eyes on Elizabeth. The flame grew. Behind the mountains, lightning flashed. A low rumble rolled over them.

"You listen to me, Marie O'Connor," Elizabeth said firmly.

"This is the only way."

"I lost Parker. I lost Dad and Mom."

"I did, too. I'm going to find them, but first I have to save a meerkat. He needs me. And there's a broken man who needs you, too. We'll save ourselves, because we're warriors, Marie. I'm a warrior and so are you. We stand and we fight."

The flame illuminated both their faces. It whipped and burned with a fury, and sparks swirled into the sky. Lightning flashed directly overhead. Thunder roared.

"I'll forget everything," Marie said, her voice almost a whisper. "Forever. Even Parker won't be able to reach me," Marie said.

"*I* will be able to reach you. Through Fede. Through his stories. We'll find each other again and remember everything. Trust me now, Marie. The stars will sing to you. Do it now," Elizabeth said. She struggled to release herself from Marie's tight grasp.

Marie opened her mouth to speak. The hair on Elizabeth's skin stood on end and a flash of heat rolled over her. The Joshua tree nearby ruptured in splinters and fire as lightning struck it.

Marie pulled back, nearly yanking Elizabeth into the roaring flame between them. She caught herself, hesitating, and her hair tangled and whipped wildly around her face. She glanced at Elizabeth.

"Now?" Marie asked.

Elizabeth nodded and mouthed the word "goodbye."

Marie released her grip.

Another bolt of lightning exploded between them. A million prism fragments spun and collided. For Elizabeth, the shattering was also a wholeness being born. Each piece of the broken world pushed against the other, as similar poles of a magnet push against themselves. They spun away into the darkness, which left only the moon, lonely and shivering in the vastness. Still, it was alive, and it spun away to find a new sun.

Chapter Twenty-Three

Back to her cage

~Federico

With a shake of her head after her own deep cough, Elizabeth finished her story. Zaagi stirred on the other side of her and yawned, having slept for several hours after the stars and moon had come out above us. We sat quietly on the park bench.

"So, shall I call you Elizabeth or Marie?"

She scowled at me.

"I'm sorry," I said.

She shook her head. "Marie is Marie. I'm Elizabeth. Perhaps we once were the same, but we are two different people now, no matter what Jamu said."

"I see."

"I think Marie is awake."

"Yes?" I sat up straight. "How is she? Can I see her?"

"She won't remember you," said Elizabeth. "She won't remember me." A single tear rolled down her cheek and she hastily wiped it away. "She won't remember who she is, and she won't remember her husband or what happened."

"And what exactly is it that happened?"

She turned to me, pleading. "He is going to take her home soon, back to her cage. He hurt her, Federico. Please, you can't let that happen ever again." She grabbed my hand. "You can give her a new life, a new beginning. You can help her to heal and keep her away from that… man."

I was flooded with a mixture of emotion, all warring within me—anger at Carl, joy that Marie was alive, hopeful that her memory would return. I was also determined to do everything I could to help her, yet fearful that I wouldn't live up to the crucial task assigned to me by this young girl.

"No. I am not the best person for this—for her. Besides, it's a decision she has to make on her own."

"She already has, Fede. Why do you think she sent me to you in the first place? I have my own life now, my own memories, and I don't belong in this world. I belong in Gichi Manidoo. Tell her my story, write it down."

I nodded. "I have, Elizabeth. I left it for her. She'll either read it or won't, and she'll make her own decisions. She's strong, you know. Stronger than me."

"Thank you." She stroked Zaagi's head distractedly, her eyes focused on the distant lake. "Can I ask you something?"

"Of course."

"What's happening? Am I real? Is Gichi Manidoo real? How can I cross between worlds so easily?" asked Elizabeth.

I took a deep breath and let it out. I reached across her and nudged Zaagi gently in his stomach with my finger. His eyes flashed open. He growled reflexively, then frowned when he realized who had poked him. "Humph," he said. He turned away, settled once again, and closed his eyes.

"Zaagi seems pretty real," I said. "And quite grumpy, I might add. Look, I don't understand everything. But I do know there are many who believe that this isn't the only world, that there may be millions, perhaps an infinite number of parallel worlds just as real as our own. Maybe they're created out of dreams, by dreamers who waltz in their sleep."

Elizabeth laughed and nodded.

"I need to heal. She needs to heal. Maybe one day…" I said.

Zaagi stopped by my feet, stood up and handed me something. I took it. It was a fat, ripe strawberry. Cool and tart, it tasted of summer and sunlight.

"Thank you," I said, chuckling. He nodded and scurried back to the bench and sat next to Elizabeth.

Elizabeth patted my hand. She stood and stopped in front of me, Zaagi by her side. She removed her dreamcatcher, raised it over my head, and placed it around my neck. The feathers and beads glowed in the darkness, illuminating our faces.

"We're going to Gichi Manidoo to find out who I am," she said quietly, looking in my eyes. Zaagi muttered something I didn't quite catch. Elizabeth smiled. "And Bellflower. We're going to find Bellflower, too. Join us when you're ready? Jamu told me cages can protect us until we're ready to be free. It's time, Fede."

"I have something I need to do, first—"

Before I could finish, she put her finger to her mouth. "Shhh. Don't say anything."

She and Zaagi walked away into the dark shadows.

Chapter Twenty-Four

De Colores

~Federico

A metallic scream rang in my ears. I shook my head and stood, my legs quivering. The front tire on the sport car I had rented, which now rested upside down, spun lazily. A flash of moonlight reflected in my eyes each time the polished rim rotated. I stumbled a few paces and collapsed in a small ravine. My breath condensed in the chilly, high desert air—small puffs that chuffed upward as my chest heaved. I let out a deep groan.

Around me, the Sangre de Cristo Mountains towered like dark sentinels. They looked familiar, but I couldn't be sure where I was—somewhere near the North Truchas Peak in the Pecos Wilderness, for I thought I recognized it in the distance. I should have known where I was, but the alcohol in my blood sloshed through my brain and numbed my senses. It made me feel dull and slow like a butter knife wrapped in a towel. My stomach lurched, and I tasted something sour on the back of my tongue. I leaned over and gagged. I smelled the intense smoke and peat of the whiskey I'd guzzled as I belched it up, and my stomach's contents splattered on the ground.

I felt my hip. The 9mm Smith and Wesson was still snug in its holster. I shifted my weight and tried to sit up. A dull throb pulsed through my buttock and up my back. I winced at the pain but was grateful nothing felt broken. I gazed at the Milky Way floating in the sky above.

"Hello, old friend," I managed to croak.

I'd left on a flight for my hometown, Santa Fe, yesterday morning. My first order of business had been to go on a binge with a few old army buddies. We'd ended up at a small cantina outside Los Alamos, drinking, shooting pool and throwing darts. I got tossed out on my ass a few hours later by a bouncer for fighting. The guy who started it was a small man with a weasel grin, a gold tooth, and a chip on his shoulder, eager to prove himself against a larger man. I'd met many like him before, and usually walked away, but this time, in my inebriated state, I gave him what he wanted.

He didn't come out of it well.

As I was speeding away, I thought I heard an ambulance siren whine behind me. Or maybe it was the police. I headed for the mountains. Pavement gave way to gravel which, in turn, gave way to a foot trail.

I wondered if Marie had read the manuscript, if Isabel had been able to give it to her. *God help me, I've let Marie down. I should have put a stop to Carl once and for all before I left.*

But then I remembered that it wasn't up to me. Maybe

she'd want to go home with him—back to her cage. That's possible, I knew. But at least if she read Elizabeth's story, she'd have a chance, she'd find another path was open to her. With no memory, she might be too deep to dig herself out ever again. *Has she read it? Which is it—was Jiibay right that it may be too late, or will the stars sing to her?*

I touched my forehead. It was like my fingers broke a dam. Blood poured into my eyes. I reached higher and gently pulled the edge of my scalp up. A fragment of glass fell on my chest. I wiped the blood from my eyes with the sleeve of my jacket.

The metallic ringing stopped and I could hear again. The silence was deafening—I yearned for the ringing to return, for its painful stab in my brain. To my right, piñon and juniper framed a spine upon which a small footpath led upward to a ragged sierra. My muscles shook as I tried to stand. Once upright, the world swayed around me. I waited for the ground to feel stable beneath my feet. After a few moments, I set out along the trail. I knew what I was looking for. Magic. I was looking for the magic I remembered from my childhood. I used to feel it when I roamed here as a young boy. So far, however, the only things that walked with me in the night's embrace were my demons.

As I limped up the path, I noticed ripe habanero chilies along the side. They don't grow wild. Someone had planted them. How strange, I thought. I bent, picked one, put it in my mouth and began to chew. Fiery needles stabbed my cheeks and tongue and brought tears to my eyes.

I rounded a bend and the pathway ended at the foot of a tall slab of smooth rock. It just ended. I remembered the stairway up the mountain that Elizabeth and Zaagi had climbed. But here, in the 'real' world, there are no stairways to take us out of our pain, no signs that point to the passage that leads to redemption or grace. I slid down to a sitting position with my back against the mountain.

I pulled the pistol from its holster and ran my finger along the barrel. I snapped the safety off and hefted the weapon—it was real and solid. I closed my eyes.

At first, the usual images came to me, the ones that chewed and threatened to swallow me every single day like I'd swallowed the habanero; Afghanistan, blood, smoke, the wide eyes of Budowski unable to scream as death pulled him down. I fought them, and instead pulled out something hiding behind the demons—my mother's eyes as she sang a lullaby, the soft black curls of her hair brushing my forehead as she leaned over me. They shone in the moonlight that seeped through a window. My body relaxed and I felt the grip on the gun loosen. I set it on the ground beside me as the song of spring's colors wafted again in my mind.

De colores, de colores es el arco iris que vemos lucir

Y por eso los grandes amores de muchos colores me gustan a mí.

But now, the only color I could see was the yellow jaundice in her eyes as she gave me what love she had left. And then even that image was gone, replaced by the needle-scabs on the inside of her arm as she tucked me in. *My little Fede, I'll meet you in the ally tomorrow and buy you warm sopapillas and honey. Mama loves you.* Then she would leave me alone and go out into the night.

I opened my eyes just in time to see a great horned owl skim the treetops, glide through a glade and disappear in shadows. I followed it with my eyes and there, in the center of the clearing, stood the reason I'd come.

Maria.

Not my Marie, of course. I'd named her after Maria in *West Side Story* because of the way the creature seemed to dance across the earth.

It was the horse I'd seen in Afghanistan. I estimated she stood sixteen hands at the withers. She wasn't a grey, but pure white with blue eyes. She pranced toward me with ears straight forward, nostrils flaring, tail up, head pointed downward on arched neck and then danced sideways. She stopped and stared directly at me.

West Side Story was the only musical I had ever seen until college. I'd saved my pennies and snuck away from Sister

Guadalupe and the other severe nuns, dumped my life's savings on the theater's ticket counter, gorged myself on popcorn, and fallen in love the way only thirteen-year-olds can.

Was Maria a symptom of illness? Had the horse I'd watched being butchered while I crouched helpless in our hole in Afghanistan, returned to haunt me? Were she and Elizabeth both hallucinations? Was she here to show me that not only was I broken inside, but that it was my own fault because I couldn't stop her from being massacred? Just like I couldn't stop the innocents I'd massacred myself?

"I couldn't save my mother. I couldn't save you. I couldn't save Marie."

Maria dropped her head, flipped it high, and made a skyward circle with her muzzle.

"I love Marie." I'd never admitted that aloud. I wasn't even sure I'd ever admitted it in my head until now.

She swished her tail and pointed her ears toward me. She spoke not a sound, but words formed clearly in my mind, resonating inside my head like the tolling of a brass bell.

Follow me.

It was time to decide. I picked up the pistol and examined it. With my other hand, I hefted the dreamcatcher that glowed on my chest.

Again, she danced sideways and turned. She glanced over her flank at me and walked away toward an early morning mist that gathered in front of her.

I set the weapon down, rose, and stepped forward into a new day.

169

Chapter Twenty-Five

Diary - 1/29/2019

~Marie

My name is Marie Mulligan, born Elizabeth Marie O'Connor, in El Paso, Texas on September 23, 1986. Or so I've learned by reading this manuscript.

It was given to me by my friend, Isabel. She told me it was written for me by a man named Federico, and that he is also my friend. It is a terrible thing to lose one's memory. But perhaps it may also be a blessing, for few people have the chance to begin again.

A man named Carl Mulligan said he is going to bring me home with him tomorrow, that I am his wife and belong with him.

I don't think I'm going to go with him. I know where I'm going.

Stories are bridges that take us where we need to go, and the truth is what I say it is.

Elizabeth and Zaagi have left for Gichi Manidoo to find her parents, and to help a beautiful, sad meerkat free his beloved Bellflower from her cage. But that decision, whether she stays or leaves, will ultimately be hers, not Elizabeth's and not Zaagi's.

I'm leaving in the morning for Santa Fe, New Mexico. Federico told me once that he found magic there as a child in the mystical mountains of Sangre de Cristo. I believe his own Gichi Manidoo will touch our world there, and that he and I will meet once again. He may be there, looking for his Marwolaeth, for I've learned from these writings that he, too, is locked in a cage of pain and anger and resentment that he's tried to bury. I had to make the decision to begin to heal myself, and he must do the same. But I will be there if he needs me as he tried to be there for me. That may be a story that I will tell in the future.

The End.

Epilogue

~Zaagitoon

"Bellflower is nearby, isn't she, Elizabeth?"

We stood in a small group of birch trees at the foot of a narrow path. The dark indigo sky above was filled with stars. The black holes were gone.

"Will she want to leave her cage?" I asked.

"Shall we find out?"

"Yes, let's." I spun in a circle and smoothed back the fur on my head with my paw. Spinning is for joy. If there were more spinning in this world, there would be far fewer cages. "And then we will find our way home, Elizabeth."

"Very well, but you have to promise me something," Elizabeth said. I looked up at her and nodded. Elizabeth reached down and took my paw in her hand. "Whatever she decides, you'll always remember the important things."

"The things of the heart."

"Yes. And that stories can set us free. Tell her a story from your heart, and she'll know what to do."

"I have an amazing story, Elizabeth," I said, whipping my tail left and right.

"I know you do. Come on, let's find Bellflower."

Down the pathway into a field of yellow daffodils, blossoming under the pale orange sky of a nearly risen sun, we walked out of the darkness. As we entered the field of flowers, four blue and pink butterflies came together and flew in a tiny circle. Elizabeth looked at me, and I looked at her. We both knew who was being reborn.

ACKNOWLEDGEMENTS

Books don't write themselves, nor do stories tell themselves. This is my first attempt. It wouldn't have happened without a lot of people's help and encouragement. I'd like to offer my enduring gratitude.

My wife, Inna Musser, who endures the journey—the highs and lows. Thanks always, love.

My editors, literary gurus, fellow prose and poetry dancers, enamored-all of storytelling's siren call, who helped to teach me the difficult craft of fiction, who read and commented on and edited various stages of the manuscript, and who shared their joy of words (to the extent I have failed to do it well, or even passably, the fault is entirely mine): Amelia Bennett; D. Michael Whelan; Courtney LoCicero; Karen Janowsky; Charlotte Courtney; Ethan Anderson; Larry Wiseman; Liv Miles; Melissa Kaye.

My friends, from work and elsewhere, for their encouragement and inspiration to keep writing; Cindy Krieger; Susan Nelson; Jennifer Chapin; Josh Cummings; many others too numerous to mention.

Elizabeth: *On ne voit bien qu'avec le cœur.*

www.ingramcontent.com/pod-product-compliance
Lightning Source LLC
Chambersburg PA
CBHW022209050726
47590CB00002B/711